# *Dakota Breezes*

by
Carol Benzel-Schmidt

*Carol Schmidt*
*Phil. 4:13*

PublishAmerica
Baltimore

© 2003 by Carol Benzel-Schmidt.
All rights reserved. No part of this book may be reproduced in any form without written permission from the publishers, except by a reviewer who may quote brief passages in a review to be printed in a newspaper or magazine.

First printing

ISBN: 1-59286-012-5
PUBLISHED BY PUBLISHAMERICA, LLLP
www.publishamerica.com
Baltimore

Printed in the United States of America

# DEDICATION

*Dedicated to the memory of my father, Fred Benzel, Jr., who was my encouragement, my mentor, my friend. Dad, I wish you could be here to enjoy this accomplishment with me! Your life-long hunger for education through reading was a wonderful role model, and even though you never knew how far-reaching your influence was, I hope to share it with you some day in heaven.*

# ACKNOWLEDGMENTS

To cousin Judy for her honest critiques, to Roy Stout for his help on South Dakota ranching and history, to Evy for her faith in my abilities. To my daughter Athena and my mother Hilda for never-ending love, and to all my friends and relatives who prodded me along the way! To my co-workers, especially Sharon, who supported me and now share in the joy of my accomplishment.

# CHAPTER ONE

"I don't know how you've kept this old heap running this long," commented the elderly mechanic as he eyed the tall slender brunette leaning against her older model car. He looked back under the raised hood and shook his head. It was a wonder the attractive young woman had managed to steer the car to the service bays before it sputtered and stopped.

"But you fixed it so I can make it another 50 miles?" Her expressive dark brown eyes were filled with apprehension.

"I can only hope," the mechanic replied, grinning while he wiped his hands on a greasy rag. "Is that as far as you have to go?"

"I'll be home then."

"Well, I sure wouldn't try to make it any farther or you'll be running on a prayer."

Dorine Andrew's face lit with a dazzling smile that made him wish he were 30 years younger. "My prayer lines to heaven are always vibrating—I couldn't have made it to and from college without a hedge of prayer around that old car!"

"Well, you'll have to get a different one if you're going back to college—this one's shot." He slammed the hood and walked toward the cluttered office, his footsteps echoing on the concrete floor.

Dorine followed, peering into the purse she had dangling from a shoulder strap. "I graduated today, so I won't be making this trip again—at least, not for college."

"Congratulations!" replied the mechanic as he picked up a pen and scribbled figures on a dog-eared receipt book. "You must live around Kadoka if you've only got 50 more miles to go."

"Close. I have a ranch out of Silverdale."

He handed her the total of the repairs and she gulped. It wasn't much compared to what the cost of a major breakdown would have been, but it would almost deplete her bank account. Boy, if Dean could see her now, he'd probably crow and say, "I told you so!" She shoved his rugged male image aside and wrote out a check on the

Circle A Ranch account.

"Thanks," the mechanic said as he briefly scanned the check before ringing up the amount on the cash register. "I did the best I could for you, but I sure wouldn't trust that old buggy any farther than Silverdale."

"I really appreciate your staying past closing time for me, because I want to get home before dark." The sun had already sunk low in the western sky when she first noticed trouble, and she'd breathed a prayer of thanks when she found this place still open. Flashing him another gracious smile, she turned and walked back to her car.

The older man leaned his forearm on the cash register, gazing after her, noting shapely legs in the modest turquoise shorts that hugged her slim hips. A long braid of thick dark hair hung down her back, swaying across the soft material of her sleeveless turquoise blouse. He sighed and turned to the register to close it for the day. He raised his hand in farewell as Dorine backed her car out of the service bay. She waved in return and pulled out towards the ramp to the westbound freeway. He hoped some lucky guy was waiting for her 50 miles down the road.

But there wasn't. No boyfriend, no special friend—not even a father or brother. The mechanic couldn't know that she never gave a thought about who would be awaiting her. As an only child, she had learned to rely on her heavenly Father through the years, and even more so after her father's death.

Thinking now only of getting home, she kept her ears open for any more strange sounds coming from under the hood. As the interstate slipped quietly away beneath her wheels, she gradually relaxed, turning her attention from car problems to enjoying the unbroken vistas of the prairie as she traveled, glad for the cooling air now that the sun was slipping down near the horizon.

However, the uneasiness that lingered at the back of her mind refused to go away, and as much as she wanted to forget, she relived once again the disturbing scene after the graduation ceremony earlier today.

Dean DeFoe and his mother, neighboring ranchers to the Circle A, had flown to her commencement in their private plane. She'd known the DeFoes all her life. Marci was her second mother...but Dean? Dean was like an older brother—an *interfering* older brother! He'd often stopped by the college during the past four years, but his visits had tapered off the past year. She inwardly cringed as she recalled why—they always ended up arguing about how he tried to run her life, but today had been the worst.

Recalling the harsh words she'd thrown at him when he insisted she junk her car and fly back home with them, she felt her face flame with embarrassment. She was determined that he would *not* dictate her actions no matter *how* well-meaning...but had he really deserved what she'd dished out?

Guilt and remorse had ridden with her all the way from the college town, nibbled at her conscience, waited in the corners of her mind.

She realized now that Dean had seen the trouble under her car hood this morning when he'd insisted on checking the oil before she started the long drive to Silverdale. But as usual, they parted in a huff when she'd told him to back off—plus a few more choice phrases.

Given her hours on the road, she'd had plenty of time to mull over her actions. She knew her belligerent attitude was not pleasing to God, and furthermore, she was a grown woman with a ranch to run. The DeFoes would always be her neighbors—she *had* to learn to get along with Dean. He and her late father had been good friends, and had traded work like all ranchers and farmers did—and she would do the same.

However, remembering the thunderous expression on his tanned face earlier, and the anger in his piercingly blue eyes, she wondered if they would *ever* get along. Neither of them wanted to budge from their positions. Taking her eyes from the freeway for a moment, she glanced out her side window at the prairie grasses undulating like ocean waves under the ever-present breezes of South Dakota. It was cooler with her window down, and she was thankful she'd braided her long hair to keep it from whipping around her face in the breeze.

Shorter strands occasionally escaped from their confinement and she darted a glance in the rearview mirror to see how wind-whipped she looked. Dark brown eyes gazed back at her, eyes framed with long dark lashes above a pert nose, full pink lips and a small chin that hinted of stubbornness. She snorted with self-derision—that stubbornness had gotten her into trouble more times than not!

She sighed and leaned her head against her upraised arm braced on the window ledge, letting her thoughts meander. They always came back to Dean. She was disgusted and tired of her brain taking a left turn just when she thought she'd forgotten her over-bearing, self-appointed guardian.

Since she had no brothers or sisters, Dean's mother often invited her to the DeFoe home. While Dean was too old to be considered a playmate, in her estimation, she'd spent many carefree hours with his younger siblings, Darrell and Darcy. But Dean had always been in the background, alternating between teasing her and scolding about the risks his siblings were exposing Dorine to—if he'd only known—*she* was the one that usually suggested the shenanigans that got them into trouble with him. Like climbing on the steep, slick metal barn roof to watch airplanes fly overhead. Now, she could understand his white face when he'd brought her down—she could have slipped and fallen, seriously injuring herself. And there had been other things, all through grade and high school.

But still, she often wondered why he bothered to visit her at the university, when he was always so disapproving of her these last few years?

A strange sound from under the hood got her immediate attention and she held her breath. *Please, Lord, just a few more miles...I know Dean was right about this car...I suspect You even sent him along but I didn't recognize Your helping hand...forgive me, Father.*

When the sound didn't reoccur, she relaxed—but her mind didn't—it immediately returned to the subject of Dean.

As a young teenager, she'd drawn herself up for battle when he'd teased about marrying her some day so he could get his hands on her ranch. She'd spat at him, "Pigs will fly before I'd marry you!"

The memories brought a slight smile to her lips, but then she sighed again. She suspected the Lord was keeping Dean in her mind because He wanted her to be His witness to him—a Dean who had turned his back on God.

She had first noticed a subtle change in him after his father had died during Dean's senior year at college. A board of directors had assisted Marci in handling the business until Dean graduated and Marci gratefully handed over the reins to her elder son.

It had been hard to see him drift from being a youth leader at church, to a stony-faced man who now refused to even attend worship. But as a child of God, she knew that Christians were used of Him to be an instrument to the lost, the hurting, the unsaved. She swallowed and frowned—it would to be hard to curb her tongue around Dean but the conviction grew stronger and stronger the closer she got to home, that she was to be that instrument.

At last, she gave in. *"Lord, I want to obey You, and I don't want to battle with Dean either every time we're together. If this is what You want of me, please give me the knowledge, grace and the words to say that will touch his cold heart."*

Following that prayer, her mind darted to her future plans—she wondered what Dean would say when he discovered her secret? Would he turn thumbs down on her plan to turn her spread into a guest ranch? There were no "dude" ranches in their area, all the other ranches were making it financially—would they resent her bringing in a commercial venture?

Signaling to pull out around a slower car, she straightened her shoulders and raised her chin—she didn't need Dean's approval to do *anything*! Her plans for the Circle A didn't have a thing to do with him. And everything to do with her own future, a future made brighter because of her father's foresightedness.

A lump formed in her throat as she thought of her late father—her friend and confidant. Her mother had died before Dorine started school, and her dad had lovingly raised her single-handedly on the Circle A, 5,000 acres of prime grasslands near the Badlands. Tears stung her eyelids and she bit her lip. What would he have done, faced with the declining economy that had plagued all ranchers and farmers the last few years? *That's why he put aside that college trust money for you,* a little voice said to her. Without the trust fund that she'd learned about only a few days before her high school graduation, she'd never have been able to go to college, even with the scholarships she'd earned.

A year ago, after she and her cousin Alfred, who had moved to the ranch to manage it while she was away at university, had gone over the ranch books, she'd known she was going to have to do something or face losing the ranch that her dad's great-grandparents had homesteaded. As always, she'd taken her burden to the Lord and after much prayer and researching, she'd decided to open her large, two-story western-styled home as a guest ranch. She'd surfed the Internet, been in touch with other guest ranches, and planned and figured until her head ached.

Now, confident that everything was in place, she could hardly wait to get home to share her ideas with Alfred and his wife Vickie. At the thought of the fastidious buxom blonde, Dorine's compassion surfaced. For as often as she'd invited Vickie to church, the older woman had always been cool to her. When Dorine had come in, hot and dirty from riding or doing chores, Vickie had turned up her fastidious little nose—she was not a typical ranch wife and Dorine often wondered what Alfred had seen in her other than looks—but they seemed to get along fine, so long as Vickie wasn't expected to work outside.

That's the only place, however, that Dorine wanted to be, riding wild and free across the range with the wind in her hair, astride Blaze, the red gelding her father had given her for her thirteenth birthday. Her free-spirited personality flourished in that setting.

A practical father, Doug had seen to it that she had a carefree childhood, and had led her to the Lord before she reached her teens. As she grew older, he also taught her responsibility. She loved learning how the ranch was run, both indoors and out, and had taken over the bookkeeping while only a freshman in high school. Now, she wondered if her dad had a premonition that something was going to happen to him because he was so adamant about her learning the ranching business. His dad, her grandfather, it was said, had worked himself to death—but Doug was much too young when his horse misstepped and thrown him into a pile of rocks where he suffered a fatal head wound.

The neighbors had gathered round her, especially the DeFoes, and a flashback brought Dean's face to mind. Even while her own grief had almost overwhelmed her, it vaguely registered that tears had threatened to spill down his tightly-controlled face at the funeral. She'd found refuge and comfort in his arms while she'd sobbed, their grief mingled in that moment and creating another bond. A poignant yearning spread through her as she remembered the safe haven of his arms, the warmth of his strong body, the deep timbre of his voice as he'd murmured softly…

She jerked her thoughts back from the "warm fuzzies," because that picture had gradually faded in the months following. Dean began to change…from being a teasing, playful friend, he'd grown into a serious, overbearing antagonist, bent on directing her every move. It was a good thing she'd had his sister and brother as a buffer.

Darcy and Darrell had a zany, cheerful view of life, and were like the siblings she never had. As youngsters, they'd clamored around in the big barns at the Double D, played hide-an-seek in the large three-story house, and swung from the branches of the tall cottonwood trees. They'd ridden forbidden calves when no one was looking and jumped from the hay mow into inviting piles of straw below; they'd gone swimming in the cattle reservoir and pretended remorse when Dean had caught them, scolding about the diseases they could catch. Adults now, Darcy was married, living in Texas, and Darrell was co-partners with Dean running the Double D…childhood was long past for any of them. And her thoughts came back again full circle to Dean. He, with the wavy dark hair and that one curl that insisted on flopping over his forehead, so that her fingers itched to push it back—oh no, not again! *Why couldn't he stay out of her mind?!!*

Letting her gaze wander over the landscape, she squelched thoughts of him by envisioning how wonderful it would be to wake up every morning in her own room, with the clear blue sky outside her window, hear meadowlarks singing, smell the freshness of alfalfa fields in bloom. She could ride Blaze out towards the Badlands just as the rising sun touched it's pink and gold fingers to the impressive deep canyons and beautiful towering rock formations. Water and wind had worn away the soil, leaving a myriad of colors in layers at which she never ceased to marvel. Even though there was little grass there, occasionally cattle would wander into the area, and Dorine had been awe-struck at the landscape as she'd ridden with her father to drive the cattle back to the grasslands. Now, she would be guiding ranch guests on that same tour, providing she could get it up and running soon.

The enormity of what she'd be undertaking sometimes seemed overwhelming, but she had prepared well. When the guest ranch idea had first occurred to her, she'd put out tentative feelers, not knowing what to expect. Therefore, she hadn't shared her ideas with anyone, not even Robin Hudson, her best friend—it would be a big project, and she wanted to have all her "ducks in a row" before she told anyone…especially a certain cowboy with intense blue eyes that could reflect humor or anger…what would he do? With exasperation, she reached over to turn up the Christian radio station—why did her brain keep asking about what Dean thought or did—he wasn't her keeper!

It suddenly registered that on the far horizon, the first signs of the Badlands were coming into view and her heart leaped with excitement—she was almost home!

A lingering shaft of sunlight touched the exit sign to Silverdale and it was like God blessing her homecoming as she exited the freeway. Braking and turning the car in the direction of Silverdale, she wondered if the landscape just seemed brighter, if the air smelled sweeter, if the song of birds was more joyous! The sleepy little town of 300 souls had closed down its businesses hours ago, except for the tavern at the edge of town—there were always mud-splattered ranch pickups parked around it like chicks gathered around a hen. Children rode their bikes on dusty streets and waved at her as she drove slowly along, savoring the familiar sights of her childhood—the feed store, post office, general store, the poolhall, hardware store, churches, the community hall where she'd learned to roller-skate one summer, houses, car repair shops, school buildings, and finally, the Sweet Schoppe café.

She slowed even more, peeking in the windows of the café to see if she could catch a glimpse of Robin, but there was no movement in the darkened interior. The little bakery-café that had been in Silverdale almost since its founding, was the local coffee place for ranchers and farmers, as well as for state workers at a nearby gravel pit. Robin opened up early and enjoyed a brisk morning business that tapered off towards evening, when she was more than happy to close and get off her feet.

Dorine would loved to have stopped, but even though the car was running smoothly, she wasn't going to push her luck—Robin would have to wait until tomorrow.

The sun had slipped below the horizon, leaving a trail of gold that reflected off the top branches of solitary cottonwoods standing sentinel by the roadside. Meadowlarks sang their evening song, perched on reeds that grew alongside irrigation ditches, and as she left the town behind, smells of the countryside wafted over her—she breathed deeply, savoring the pure fresh air of the prairie.

Following the narrow asphalt road that dipped and wound its way towards the Badlands, Dorine tried to tamp down her excitement, but the knowledge that she'd never have to leave the ranch again almost made her giddy!

Driving by the impressive paved entryway to the DeFoe Ranch, she noted early summer flowers were blooming in the painstakingly-designed landscaping around the sign stating that this was the home of DeFoe Enterprises. She knew the latest addition was a large, covered arena under construction, one that could host 4-H events, cattle and horse shows even in the winter if it wasn't too cold. She'd have to go over to see it…later.

Rounding the next bend, she slowed and turned right, rattling across the metal cattle guard under the large overhead ranch sign with the Circle A brand. The long, graveled dusty road to the ranch buildings wound through acres of her land, and as she came over a ridge, she could see ahead how the house chimney appeared to be nestled among branches of the tall cottonwoods that surrounded the homestead. Even though she drove slowly, the tires left a familiar dusty trail billowing out behind her—one of these days, she'd have to do something about this road.

But for now, she couldn't wait to get into the house, greet her cousins, then unload her car, shower and snuggle down in her own bed, just like the birds that soared and glided overhead, drifting towards the trees for the night. All of creation was saying goodnight, with the sky pulling down shades of pastel pink and lavender on the window of the world.

Anticipation mounted as she drove around the last curve, but something caught her eye—had Vicki planted yellow flowers in front of the house? Coming to the top of the rise leading into the yard, her heart almost stopped and she took her foot off the accelerator—the yellow she'd glimpsed was not flowers, but police barricade tape strung all around the front of the house.

# CHAPTER TWO

Letting the car coast to a stop, Dorine hardly noticed when the engine gave out a final cough and died. Automatically switching off the key, she sat in stunned silence, trying to take in the sight before her. Her heart was pounding and filled with dread, but she willed herself to open the door and get out.

A few cranky sounds escaped from under the hood as the engine cooled, then silence pressed in around her. She glanced towards the barns and corrals—everything seemed deserted and for the first time in her life, Dorine felt a strange sort of fear as she stood in the yard of the only home she'd ever known. Where was Vicki? Alfred, she knew, could still be out working somewhere, but there was no sign of *anyone*. Where were the ranch hands? Evening shadows were stealthily taking over the yard, softening the outline of the trees and adding to the unearthly silence.

Slowly, she approached the yellow barrier tape, ducked under it and walked along the paving-stone sidewalk, her shoes barely making a sound. She went up the wide steps onto the verandah and stopped in front of the door with antique beveled glass. Her heart pounded harder and her palms grew sweaty, but she grasped the knob and bravely pushed open the door.

The sight that greeted her was like something out of a horror movie—furniture was overturned, garish paint had been splattered on every wall, fixtures were torn down and doors had been ripped off. Windows were broken and dust covered everything.

She leaned against the door, a sob catching in her throat. *What had happened? Did the whole house look like this?*

Her heart pounding until it throbbed in her ears, she carefully stepped through the debris, peering into the kitchen and moaning at the sickening sight of once-gleaming white appliances that had been smashed. On weak legs that threatened to give out under her, she turned and picked her way across broken glass towards the stairway, noting fresh gouges in the dark polished wood. With one foot on the steps, she looked upward, but couldn't bring herself to climb the stairs.

The sound of an approaching vehicle penetrated her numbness. It was an effort to turn and make her way slowly back to the front door. She stopped and ventured a look into the living room—her beloved old piano had been attacked, with the keys sticking up at odd angles…discolored patches showed on the wall where pictures had hung… the glass on the front of the bookcases lay shattered on the floor. And over all, the unnatural quiet.

She stumbled to the front door, pulled it open and stepped out, expecting to see Alfred's old battered pickup. But it was Dean getting out of his car. He slammed the door and reached up to pull his sunglasses off as he gazed at her, a serious expression on his rugged features that were shadowed under the brim of his straw hat. Gone were the dress clothes of this morning—he wore his usual blue cotton work shirt and washed-out jeans with frayed cuffs draped over scuffed cowboy boots.

"Did you…know…about…this?" she asked hoarsely, moving to the porch railing to lean heavily against it.

He nodded before ducking under the tape, then straightened to watch her intently. It almost tore him apart to see the shocked disbelief on her lovely features, and he took a step toward her.

She turned away from him, raising one hand to cover her mouth with slim fingers while her gaze roamed over her beloved home. A wave of despair swept through her, sobs welled up and her eyes filled with tears. A strangled sound escaped and her control deserted her.

Suddenly, it didn't matter that Dean was the enemy— at this moment, he represented solid familiarity in a world that had suddenly gone crazy. Turning blindly towards him and rushing down the steps, she threw herself into his waiting arms.

He held her tightly, crooning soothing words as he laid his cheek on the top of her head, breathing in her familiar floral scent. His sunglasses dangled from one finger as he splayed his hand, then began to trace circles on her back.

"Why would anyone do this?" she cried as she pressed herself closer against his broad chest. "My house! My beautiful house!" He silently offered her comfort and security, gritting his teeth as he squeezed his eyes shut tight, wanting to take her pain.

*Lord, how he loved this woman!* He couldn't remember a time he didn't love her—he had lost his little boy heart to her as he watched her baby triumph in sitting up by herself for the first time, clapping her tiny hands. Even then, she exhibited an independent spirit. When she had taken her first faltering steps, it had been from her mother to him that she toddled; he had taught her to ice skate, he had helped her perfect her roping skills, and when she was in high school, he'd had to restrain himself as he watched her through her first throes of puppy love with that Marshall kid. He'd agonized the four long years when she was away at college, hoping she wouldn't fall in love with some computer geek who would take her away from the life that he wanted for her.

Now, she was here, safe in his arms, and he tucked her more closely against his chest, burying his nose in her sweetly-perfumed hair. "Oh, my poor little sweetheart," he murmured softly—then realizing he'd spoken out loud, he tensed, hoping she hadn't heard him. With her prickly pride and stubbornness, he didn't want to ruin everything by alienating her with a few unguarded words!

As the storm of sobs gradually subsided, Dorine became aware of the warm arms around her, the comforting sound of his steady heartbeat and the fragrance of pine scent mingled with horse and leather smells—this was as familiar as home…this was Dean. She grew quiet and rested against him, wanting to burrow her head deeper to hide from the unreal world into which she'd stumbled.

She was too upset and deep in misery to understand what he'd whispered, but when he tensed, his body language plainly told her that he did *not* appreciate her crying all over him, no matter *how* familiar he was! Suddenly embarrassed at her outburst, she stiffened, chagrined at her naiveté in assuming that he would want her clinging to him. Especially after the way she'd talked to him today!

Drawing back, she covered the awkward moment by blurting out, "I'm getting your shirt all wet!" She made futile attempts to wipe the wet spot away while his arms remained loosely around her waist.

He chuckled softly, his deep voice vibrating from within his broad chest, the sound making strange sensations up and down her spine. "It'll dry." He raised one hand to catch her nervous fingers, holding them still, and she felt the calluses caused by the hard physical work he did—he may run a multitude of businesses from his hi-tech office, but he preferred working outdoors alongside his ranch hands. She stared at his darkly-tanned fingers holding her own slender white hand. Strange, she'd never noticed how strong and capable his hands were...and since when had touching him like this made her fingers feel so...so...sensitive?

"I know what a shock this must be, prairie chick." At the use of his pet name for her, her eyes misted over again, and she slowly relaxed, her fingers resting in his. Childhood scenes replayed through her mind, back to the time when as a small child, he'd found her hiding during a party at his parent's house, too shy to come out with strangers there. That's when he'd nicknamed her "prairie chick," for the timid little bird that hid in the wild grasses of the plains.

Later, when he'd teased about marrying her and she'd yelled at him, he would respond with that deep laugh that seemed to come from his very soul, and his blue eyes would darken with merriment. His mother would cluck gently and chide him for teasing Dorine, but he dismissed her scolding and continued his teasing.

Now, she felt the warmth of remembrance being replaced with numbness. A hooty-owl sounded its distinctive cry in the distance, emphasizing the loneliness she felt clear to her bones, in spite of Dean's arms having held her so tenderly.

She took a deep breath to steady herself and gently pushed away from him, absently swatting at a buzzing mosquito. This was *her* problem, not his. She reminded herself that she was a confident woman who could handle her own challenges.

Dean sensed her gathering strength—it was one of the things he admired about her. She may get knocked down by life's blows, but she always bounced back. "I was going to be here when you got home, but a mare was having trouble giving birth and I was in the barn longer than I figured....I'm sorry that you had to walk into this alone." He slapped at a mosquito on his neck, irritated at the insect.

She slowly turned away, tucking her fingers into the front pockets of her shorts to keep from hanging on to him. Ducking under the yellow tape, she leaned against the front of her car, looking up at the house. "What happened? When? Why didn't you tell me? You knew about it all along, didn't you?" Of *course* he knew—this would have been front-page news in a community this small!

He followed behind her, ducking under the tape to stand beside her. "I was afraid that you'd drop everything, come home, and risk not graduating," he stated simply. He longed to hold her while they talked, but had to content himself with her by his side. He leaned back against the car, crossed his arms over his chest and stared up at the house too. "It happened a few weeks ago—"

"—But why didn't someone let me *know?!!*" Dorine demanded, her dark eyes imploring as she impatiently brushed away mosquitoes.

His gaze lowered slowly to her ravaged face. "You wouldn't have stayed to take your finals, Dorine. You know you would have hot-footed it home and tried to do something here all by yourself."

She opened her mouth to protest, then closed it again—he was right, that's exactly what she would have done. He curved his hand around her shoulder, pulling her to his side. Warm prickles ran down her arm. He continued, "Alfred and Vicki had gone back East for a few days, and when they returned, this is what they found. The house is pretty much trashed, Dorine, it can't be lived in, so Vicki moved into Rapid City and Alfred is staying in one of the bunkhouses." He frowned, turning to look in that direction. "It's odd he's not here—he knew you were coming home today, didn't he?"

She nodded. His quiet, matter-of-fact tone helped to calm her, stabilize her tilting world. "We've talked by phone, and I sent an announcement, but he told me they couldn't come for graduation."

At her last words, anger darkened Dean's expression. *How could they not support her*? A mosquito, sinking its proboscis deep into his skin, fueled his anger and he swatted it viciously, blooding his arm.

He'd never understand that cold-hearted Vicki!

Her gaze returned to the house. "Everything is in such a mess." She slumped in defeat, leaning more heavily against the car and whispered, "Wh-what am I going to do?" She waved her hand to brush the mosquitoes away that were dancing in front of her face.

He straightened and said brusquely, "For right now, why don't you come over to our place? You can stay in Darcy's old room until you decide what to do…and by the way, since we've got the same insurance company, Alfred and I have been able to work together on this. I talked the insurance investigator into letting me take your clothes and personal belongings out of your room. They're stored over at our place."

His authoritative tone used to make her hackles rise and she'd dig in her heels. Now, it didn't matter, because her future was bleak—it looked as though all her plans for the guest ranch were down the tube.

"Come on, you can ride with me and come back for your car tomorrow. You're tired out from driving all afternoon—and if we don't hurry up, these mosquitoes will eat us alive!"

She nodded and turned slowly, all the fight gone out of her. Deepening shadows were slowly turning into a soft warm night, with a half-moon on the horizon. This was the time of evening when the almost constant Dakota breezes died away, leaving a hush over the land and over her soul. Birds had quieted after twittering above in the tree as they settled for the night, and the ever-present hungry buzzing of mosquitoes was joined in a serenade of frogs from down in the drain ditch. But even the familiar sounds of home couldn't erase her sense of loneliness—she was in this by herself.

Dean hated to see her so dejected, and stepped quickly around her to open the door, helping her in. *Even if she didn't realize it, she needed him right now.* He hoped to make her need him more in the coming days, but for now, he knew he had to watch his step carefully—she wouldn't remain in this submissive mood for long!

His caring attitude was her undoing and she dissolved in tears again after getting into the car. As he opened the door on the driver's side, she tried to pull herself together, but she couldn't seem to stop the flood of tears. He got in and instead of starting the engine, leaned across the console to put his arms around her.

"Don't cry, little one, it's going to be all right," he murmured, his lips brushing her ear. She only cried harder, leaving him feeling helpless. "You're just tired and probably hungry—" he put a knuckled finger under her chin, turning her toward him. "When did you last eat?"

She blinked and thought as she raised tear-drenched eyes to him. "I...I guess it was the last time I stopped...." He brushed a tear from her long lashes with one finger, but restrained himself from planting a kiss on those beautiful, kissable lips—she'd probably deck him! It tore his heart to see her so distressed—and not be able to help.

"And what did you eat? A candy bar? Some ice cream?" he demanded, more gruffly than he intended.

She guiltily lowered her eyes.

His breath hissed out slowly. "Dorine, you know better—" he stopped. *She didn't need scolding now, she needed loving.* Letting go of her and turning to start the car, he said, "Well, it doesn't matter, we'll be home in a few minutes and Mrs. Mac can get you something."

"Oh, but it's so late—"

He slanted a glance in her direction as he backed the car up and started out of the yard. "Are you kidding? As soon as Mrs. Mac finds out you're home and haven't eaten, she'll scold you a lot worse than anything *I* could ever say!"

A ghost of a smile touched her lips and a little light came back into her dull eyes at the mention of Mrs. Mac, the DeFoe's housekeeper. Actually, she was more like a member of the family, it was ridiculous to think of her as a housekeeper when she was so much a part of the family.

As Dean's smooth-riding car carried them towards his ranch, she slipped down into the comfortable seat and felt the tenseness draining out of her. She vaguely realized in passing, that for the first time in many years, she was letting Dean take charge...willingly.

# CHAPTER THREE

Seated at the DeFoe's big oak table in the spacious kitchen, Dorine felt a measure of comfort as Marci slid a cup of hot tea in front of her, sitting down beside her. Marci and Mrs. Mac had welcomed her with enthusiasm that had quickly changed to concern when they saw how devastated she was, both expressing gratitude to Dean for bringing her to them.

Mrs. Mac, a buxom woman with dark, sharp eyes that never missed a thing, had a head of white hair worn in soft waves swept into a bun at the back. As a child, Dorine had been in awe of that beautiful hair—it reminded her of royalty.

Now, Mrs. Mac bustled between the stove and refrigerator, putting together an omelet. She clucked over this thin neighbor child who had turned into a lovely young woman—who, in spite of having a college education, didn't have sense enough to eat properly or on time!

Dorine would have protested the kind woman's efforts to feed her, but the day's events were too raw, and she submissively let Dean suggest that Mrs. Mac "get something inside this girl before she blows away." He had left her with his mother and Mrs. Mac while he went to his den down the hall.

"Dear, this is most certainly not the homecoming we had envisioned for you," gently began Marci. A tall slender woman, Marci carried herself with a natural gracefulness and a kind spirit that endeared her to all who knew her. Her eyes rested tenderly on the down-cast head of this dear little lamb. "You *will* stay here, now that you've seen you can't stay at your house?"

"I...I don't...know...," Dorine whispered, raising her head. "My mind is almost blank...I still can't believe what's happened." She paused, her voice soft. "God has promised that He won't allow anything more in our lives than we can handle...but I don't know how to handle this." She raised misty eyes to Marci.

"This is one of those testing times," Marci replied softly, putting her hand over Dorine's. "God gives strength for each trial as you face it, not before, and all in His good time."

Dorine felt the comfort flowing from the older woman's touch, sending warmth into her cold fingers. Nodding, she pulled one hand free to reach for her cup. Taking a sip, she felt the warm liquid slide down her dry throat as she let her eyes roam around the large airy room that was the hub of this caring family. Here they gathered for meals, played cards, drank coffee with neighbors. Cabinets and a pantry off to the right of the entry were stocked with enough supplies to carry them through weeks of blizzards in the winter. It was a long way to the grocery store, and Mrs. Mac made sure there were ample provisions— she reigned undisputed in "her" kitchen.

There were wall ovens, a cook top and grill, large upright freezer, and plenty of counter space where she mixed dough for breads, cakes and pies. A large window above the sink overlooked the swimming pool and kept her in touch with the outdoors.

Mrs. Mac stood now with her hands planted on her ample hips, her dark gaze troubled as she studied Dorine. Then she turned to her omelets, whipping eggs to a froth with a fork in a large blue bowl that Dorine remembered was the older woman's favorite. "God sometimes has mysterious ways to accomplish His purpose. We don't understand His ways, they're not our ways and we may never understand this side of heaven," she remarked, her hands keeping up a rhythm with the words. Glancing up over her rimless glasses, she added, "That's from the Good Book…remember, Dorine?"

"Isaiah, chapter 55," Dorine replied, knowing Mrs. Mac expected her to remember her Sunday school teaching.

"We have a graduation party planned for you this weekend, dear," Marci said, "just some of your friends and a few neighbors, but maybe you'd rather not have it, after all that's happened?"

Dorine's eyes misted over again at the thoughtfulness of this kind woman. She blinked rapidly. "I don't know why I feel like crying all of a sudden—it seems that's all I've done for the past two hours!"

Marci leaned over and put her slender hand on Dorine's arm. "My dear, you've had a terrible shock," she hesitated, "but if you don't feel up to having a party—"

"Oh no, it's not that," Dorine hastily assured her, "it's just that…everything is happening so fast! You've probably gone to a lot of trouble already, and I can't change the way things are—my house is still in a mess, and I'm told I can't live there." She wiped a tear.

"Mrs. Mac and I *love* parties!" Marci smiled fondly at her friend Maple. Marci never used her first name— "Mrs. Mac" seemed so much more appropriate and respectful for the older woman, the title in keeping with her regal bearing. "We'll barbecue and swim."

"Thank you, Marci," Dorine replied gratefully. "I never even thought about a party…I was so eager to get home and get on with my plans"—she stopped abruptly, overcome with emotion.

"You will stay here, won't you, dear?" Marci repeated anxiously.

Swallowing around the lump in her throat, Dorine leaned over to hug Marci. "I can't even think straight right now. It's so kind of you to offer…yes, I'll stay. I don't really have a choice, do I? There's no where else to go."

"Well, then, that's settled," Marci replied, embracing her in return.

Dorine drew back and took the tissue Marci handed her. "The first thing I need to do is find out about the insurance. Dean said he was working with Alfred on it, but all the paperwork is over at my house…or maybe it was destroyed too?"

Marci replied softly, "Why don't you ask Dean about it? I put your clothes and personal items up in Darcy's room, but he has everything else. I don't know all the details."

"There's been a lot of talk about strange things happening around here lately," added Mrs. Mac, dumping the eggs into a sizzling hot pan and stirring vigorously. "Land a mercy!" she muttered.

Their conversation was interrupted by the loud roar of a high-powered vehicle, and Mrs. Mac rolled her eyes. "*That boy*! When is he *ever* going learn that driveway isn't a race track!"

The engine cut off and the slamming of a door was followed by booted footsteps hurrying up the walk. The outer screen door opened with a squeak then clapped shut. A moment later, a tall, lanky, dark-haired young man—a younger version of Dean— stepped through the kitchen door, a satisfied grin on his handsome face when his hat landed on a wall peg. He turned and spotted Dorine— "Yee-haw! Don't tell me *Cowgirl* is here?!!"

"Darrell! You old sheepherder!" Dorine exclaimed as she rose to her feet. Her heart lifted at the sight of her child-hood friend. In two strides, he reached her, picking her up and swinging her around. "You'll be so dang smart a feller won't be able to stand you, now that you've got your edukashun!" he exclaimed.

"Darrell! Stop using slang!" Marci scolded good-naturedly as she smiled at his exuberance. Mrs. Mac rolled her eyes again, shaking her head.

Darrell set Dorine on her feet, holding her loosely with his linked hands behind her back. "It's good to have you home," he said sincerely, and surprised her by leaning down to kiss her forehead. Marci glanced at Mrs. Mac and a look passed between them.

At that moment, Dean came into the room and stopped short, his eyes narrowing at his brother's arms around Dorine. Darrell turned and laughed. "It seems like just a few years ago that we were trundling her around in the wagon, now she's all grown up and come home to stay—you *are* here to stay, aren't you?" he turned back to her. "No more running off to Europe or wherever?"

A knife-sharp pain pierced Dean's heart as he yanked his gaze to her—*he'd never thought about her going anywhere else*! Had she told Darrell she wasn't staying at Silverdale? A fear greater than he'd ever known clutched his chest while he waited for her answer.

Dorine smiled and disentangled herself from Darrell, then glanced at Dean, who continued to stare at her. "No, I'm not going anywhere." She looked puzzled. "Where would I go? Silverdale is my home, my roots are buried deep here in Dakota...and," she glanced shyly at Marci, "your mother has invited me to stay...to be a pain in your neck..." she let her sentence trail off slyly.

She couldn't know the relief that flooded through Dean as he heard her familiar teasing of his brother. Her spunk was returning.

Darrell moaned, leaned his head back and covered his eyes with one hand. "Oh no! You mean I have to put up with *you*?!!" She elbowed him and he doubled up in mock distress.

Mrs. Mac hurried to the table with a plate of food, gesturing for Dorine to sit down while sending dark looks in Darrell's direction.

"Eat it," Dean said softly as he walked past Dorine, heading for the coffee pot. She glared at him when he slid a sideways look at her.

Moving closer as he leaned towards her, Darrell whispered loudly, "You better eat it, or he'll hand feed you!"

"He better not try!" she retorted, with some of her old spirit.

"Just eat it," Dean repeated, glancing at her, then the plate.

"I...I can't, with you watching my every move!" she snapped.

He chuckled softly. "Get a good night's rest, prairie chick, then come over to the office in the morning and we'll talk." She glanced up at him, but his eyes were unreadable. She nodded and looked down at her plate as he walked back down the hall. Darrell brushed past her, squeezing her shoulder affectionately before he bounded up the stairs to his room.

While she ate, Marci chatted easily with her, catching her up on the latest news. Mrs. Mac ran water into the sink to wash the pan, occasionally adding her comments.

Later, Dorine accompanied Marci to the second floor bedroom that had been Darcy's. She'd spent many a night here, and the familiar scene wrapped around her like a warm blanket—at least this had not changed. The decor was intact from Darcy's high school days, pink and white being the main color theme. Marci crossed to the dresser and rummaged in one of the drawers. "Here, this should fit you, you girls are almost the same size." She held out one of Darcy's old nightgowns and Dorine took it gratefully. Marci glanced around. "I don't think there's anything else I need to tell you, the bathroom is still through there," she nodded toward a closed door to the right, "and the towels are still in the same place."

Dorine hugged her again. "Thank you so much, Marci. You've made me feel so much better...and so welcome."

Marci returned the hug, drawing back to look at the young woman who was by all intents, her second daughter. "Your mother was my best friend, honey, and I'd do *anything* for you. You're sweet and precious in your own right, but every time I look into those dark brown eyes of yours, I see Amy...and I know she would be pleased that I can be here for you."

Dorine's eyes misted. "I hardly remember her, but thanks to you and Daddy, her memory has been kept alive for me."

Marci patted her on the arm. "You get a good night's rest, honey, and we'll see you in the morning. I usually go out in the garden while it's still cool, but Mrs. Mac will be in the kitchen to fix your breakfast. Good night."

"Good night...and thanks again." The door closed behind Marci.

After a hot shower, Dorine sat on the edge of the quilt-covered bed, running a comb through her long hair. A well-worn Bible was laying on the nightstand and she opened it to the New Testament. She'd always relied on the Scriptures to comfort her, no matter what the circumstances or how tired she was. Going to her favorite verse, Philippians 4:13, she read the encouraging words: *I can do all things through Christ who strengthens me.* Closing her eyes, she dwelled on the promise that Jesus will give us strength when we need it—not before and not after—right at the precise moment. She reverently closed the Bible and put it back, then slid in between the fresh-smelling white sheets.

*How strange life is...this morning I had the world by the tail, all my plans made, and tonight, I don't even have a home...*her eyes focused on the posters of teen idols that were still pinned on the ceiling...she wondered if Marci had left them on purpose, so when Darcy's twin daughters were older and came to visit, they would lay in this bed and laugh over their mother's long-ago "dream hunks."

After switching off the bedside lamp, her eyes adjusted to the darkness. Soft moonlight spread silvery patterns on the carpeted floor and across the end of her bed. Jumbled scenes from today played through her mind...*the graduation ceremony where she had received the most inspirational award...the shock of seeing paint splattered all over her living room...heart-wrenching good-byes to college friends she'd known for four years...Dean's scowl when he'd asked her to go home with them and she'd refused, then the warm comfort of his arms this evening...Marci's gentle expressions...Dean's tenderness when he'd called her "prairie chick"...her car...the heavy beat of his heart when he'd held her...Heavenly Father, I'm so mixed up, please be with me tonight and in the coming days. Reveal to me the purpose behind the troubles that have come upon me...I give it all to You...and God? Help me to show Your love to Dean, help me demonstrate the love I have for You. In Jesus precious name, Amen.*

Her last conscious moments were spent, as they were every night, in sweet fellowship with her Lord as she poured out her heart to Him. A calmness crept over her and she slept peacefully.

# CHAPTER FOUR

Weak rays of early morning sunshine streaming in her windows wakened her and for a moment, she lay there, disoriented. Then everything came flooding back, and she sat up. The memory of the ugly mess in her house was there to taunt her and she was thankful she'd established a morning ritual to get her day started off right: "Today, God, there isn't anything You and I can't handle." She sighed, her eyes coming to rest on the suitcases sitting on the floor just inside the door—how did *they* get here? She'd left all her things in her car, parked in front of her house—*of course*, there was only *one* person who would have done this! For a moment, indignation threatened to overwhelm her, then she was reminded of her vow yesterday and the feeling drained away—she only hoped she could *maintain* her new attitude!

Her clothes were hung neatly in the closet, with boots and shoes arranged underneath. She wondered how she would ever be able to repay Marci for all her kindness and hospitality...*and let's not forget Dean*, whispered that little voice in her mind. She was so in the habit of bristling at him, that she suddenly realized it was going to be hard to break that habit, to *be* a good witness to Dean. Sighing, she got up to face her first day at the DeFoes, wondering what the coming hours held for her.

As she dressed in soft, well-worn jeans, boots and a sleeveless plaid cotton blouse, she thought of her upcoming conversation with Dean. Brushing and braiding her hair to one plait down her back, she reviewed the questions she had for him. Touching her lips with a light pink lipstick and wiping her hands down the sides of her jeans, she felt ready to face the day, whatever it might bring.

Wonderful aromas of coffee and bacon drifted up the stairs as she walked down the hall. Passing Dean's room, she glanced in then stopped short—the picture she'd given the DeFoes when she graduated from high school was sitting in a silver frame on his nightstand. Her hand crept up to her throat—why did *he* have it? She took a deep breath and started slowly down the steps. Could it really be possible he *missed* his "kid sister"?

In the kitchen, Darrell was just getting up from the table, and stealing a last sip of coffee, raised his eyebrows at her. "Good morning!" she warbled.

He was dressed for work as always, disreputable jeans, dusty boots and blue chambray shirt. Setting the cup down, he stooped to grab his old battered straw hat off the floor. "Good morning! Man, you look a lot more chipper this morning than you did last night!"

She wrinkled her nose at him as she crossed the wide expanse of the kitchen to pour herself a cup of coffee. "Did I look that bad?"

He stopped in the act of cramming the hat on his head, looked thoughtfully at the ceiling and scratched his chin. "If you have to think that hard, don't break your brain over it!" Dorine laughed as she leaned against the counter. Good old Darrell, he hadn't changed—he was one of the bright spots she'd missed. Mrs. Mac came bustling out of the pantry and gave a reassuring nod to Dorine, then turned to Darrell. "And *you*! You better be here on time for dinner today!"

"Yes, Ma'am!" Darrell saluted her, winked at Dorine and left.

Mrs. Mac shook her head and went to the breadboard where a mound of white dough awaited her. "That boy! He needs to get a wife!" she mumbled. "Him and his sassy ways!"

"He hasn't changed any," Dorine agreed. She secretly thought that Darrell must be Mrs. Mac's favorite, the way she fussed at him. She never called *Dean* "that boy," or scolded about *him* being on time for meals! Now, she motioned Dorine to the table, and after dishing up her breakfast, Dorine ate enough to satisfy the older woman. Carrying her dishes to the sink, Dorine sighed contentedly. "Good as ever, Mrs. Mac!" The older woman's face beamed as she watched Dorine rinse the dishes and put them in the dishwasher. "I'm going over the office, Dean said he wanted to see me this morning."

Busy pummeling the bread dough, Mrs. Mac waved a floured hand toward the door. "Just so you remember—dinner is at twelve sharp!" Dorine laughed as she let the screen door clap shut behind her.

Crossing the combination sunroom/washroom, she stopped short when she saw boxes from her car piled on the cement floor. Irritation at Dean's interference bubbled up— she appreciated getting her clothes, but what right did he have to unload her car? Her promise to God was getting harder and harder to keep!

Walking rapidly out into dappled sunlight, she hesitated when she noticed her car near the garage. Realization hit her smack between the eyes and her temper began to soar—*that did it!* That big cowboy was assuming just too much!

A pair of legs protruded from under the car. "Steve, is that you?" she snapped.

A muffled voice replied. "Hi, Dorine!" Steve Marshall had been her high school heartthrob, and was now the ranch mechanic. "Dean asked me to check out your car—" there was a bang— "but I can't even get it started! How long have you been drivin' it like this—" another bang.

Dorine's temper went up another notch—she didn't have money to pay for car repairs. "Don't do any more until I tell you, Steve."

There was silence for a moment. "But Dorine, Dean told me to wo—"

"Never mind what he said, it's *my* car and *I* decide what's to be done. I'll talk to you later." With a full head of steam, she turned and marched towards the towering cottonwoods bordering a smooth asphalt road that divided the ranch complex. Noise from cattle, trucks and the occasional airplane were only muffled sounds at the house with the buffer of trees and lilac bushes. The scent of the many shades of lavender and purple flowers hung heavy in the air, but for once, she didn't even notice—she had somebody to straighten out!

Turning the corner of the nearest building, the well-planned complex hardly registered on her this morning. Buildings, fences and walkways fit into the prairie landscape as though placed there by the Creator, showing thoughtful care in design. Just beyond the last corral, the skeleton of the new arena was raising up into the clear blue Dakota sky, as workmen scurried around like so many ants. Beyond it was the small airstrip with a hanger where Dean's plane was stored.

Taking a deep, calming breath, however, she remembered Dean wouldn't be the only one in the office—a half dozen cars were parked in the area marked "employees." She put a pleasant expression on her face and pushed through the impressive entry to the business office, greeted by a welcome rush of air-conditioning. Since she had last been here, Dean had made this the headquarters for DeFoe Enterprises, enlarging this space and adding several more workstations. DeFoe Enterprises encompassed not only this home ranch with its working herd and rodeo stock, but several ranches in Oklahoma and Texas, as well as a chain of western wear stores all across the South.

Dean's plump, middle-aged secretary glanced up from her front desk, her jovial face breaking into a wide smile when she saw Dorine. Her gray eyes twinkling, Hazel Brown rose and came around her desk. "Good morning, Dorine!" She enveloped the young woman in a bear hug, then stepped back. "It's so good to have you home," but her smile faded as she added, "I'm so sorry, honey, about what happened to your house."

Dorine's irritation evaporated at Hazel's warm greeting. How could she remain angry in the face of this bubbly woman? "It *is* wonderful to be back." She turned to the other secretaries, "Hi, Loretta, Darlene!—it's great to see you guys!" The two women had been several years ahead of Dorine in school, and welcomed her with heart-felt congratulations on her graduation.

"Before you get too involved with catching up on the news, come on in here first, Dorine!" Dean spoke from his office door. As she moved toward him, she suddenly experienced a wave of self-consciousness. *Why am I so nervous? It's just Dean!* She stepped past him, the scent of his cologne tickling her nose and causing funny flutters in her stomach.

His carpeted office was in sharp contrast to his den at the house. There, the room was designed for comfort and relaxing, in shades of brown and green—here, everything was sleek and modern—with no hint of relaxing. Computers sat to one side at a cluttered workstation next to a FAX machine, and another wall was lined with file cabinets. Dean's paper-strewn, black-topped desk dominated the room—*much as he's tried to do to me*, she muttered to herself.

He followed her in, closing the door behind him. Noting her raised eyebrow, he grinned wryly. "They don't need to know everything." Moving behind his desk, he shuffled papers he'd been working on. "How did you sleep?!" He drank in her fresh, dark beauty, hardly believing that she was finally here, here in Dakota to stay. And in his employ, if his plan worked, where he could be near her every day, keeping an eye on her. The prospect almost caused him to drop his guard.

She shoved her fingers in the front pockets of her jeans, glancing away from his inquiring gaze. "I...I slept good...but I didn't appreciate you bringing my car over here and unloading it without asking me. I'll just have to put everything back when I go home."

He gazed at her, unruffled. "It wouldn't start this morning, and if it has to be put in the shop, it's better not to have all your stuff in it...besides, you were still sleeping, I couldn't ask you."

"To be real blunt, Dean, I don't have money for car repairs. How come you told Steve to work on it without asking me?"

He dropped into his chair and it squeaked in protest. Picking up a pencil, he tapped it on the desk before answering her. Actually, she was right—Darrell had warned him not to crowd her, that she was a grown woman who could make her own decisions—but to him, she was still his little "prairie chick"...however...

"You're right, I should have...I was just trying to be helpful."

His capitulation took the wind out of her sails. Pretending to study the many pictures and plaques on the wall, she moved restlessly, then turned to him. In a softer voice, she said, "I didn't really come over here about my car. Before I do anything else, I have to talk to Alfred. What did you want?" *There was that wayward curl again...*

He leaned back in the well-worn swivel chair. "Two things actually. You know about the rustling down in Nebraska awhile back?" She nodded and he went on. "We think they may be here."

"Here on the Double D?" Dorine squeaked in disbelief as she

lowered herself into one of the black guest chairs.

Dean leaned forward, resting his forearms on the desk. "All over the county, several counties in fact...and we think the vandalism at your house may be tied in with that."

"But what does cattle disappearing have to do with vandalism?"

"Nothing, at first glance. But no one missed any more cattle after your house was trashed. At first, we thought the missing cattle were the usual thing, coyotes, or losing some in a blizzard, or they just strayed off. But no one could ever find any evidence of where they'd gone. If it had been coyotes, there would have been hides and bones, the same with blizzards, there would have been some evidence. And even if they'd strayed, they'd eventually have turned up in someone's pasture. When we started comparing stories, that's when we began to suspect rustlers."

"Did Alfred and I lose any?...he hasn't said a word!"

Dean nodded. "And we did too, from the ranch herd, but nothing from the rodeo stock. It's sure funny, though, after your house was trashed—no more missing cattle. It may have been that whoever was doing this got wind of the fact that we'd started night watches, and the state police were patrolling more frequently. Anyway, the insurance company is trying to determine if the two are connected."

"But why *my* house?" Dorine questioned in a quavering voice. Dean glanced at her then took a deep breath to quell his anger at the unknown vandals and the trauma they'd caused her.

"Maybe because they knew Alfred and Vicki weren't home at the time; maybe they were getting bored and impatient...who knows?" He paused. "Anyway, the investigator doesn't want the evidence to be disturbed until they get to the bottom of this. It could just have been a bunch of delinquent teens out for a joyride."

"In the meantime, what am *I* supposed to do?" she asked more to herself than to him. "If I can't even live at the ranch, how am I supposed to run it?" He had no way of knowing she was thinking of the guest ranch, plans that were now like smoke wisps in the wind.

"Well, you know you're welcome to stay here. Vicki seems to be happy right where *she* is...I don't think she ever really liked living so far out here anyway."

Dorine couldn't believe they were having a calm discussion and she sneaked a suspicious look at him. He sounded so relaxed, but she knew that shrewd mind was constantly in motion.

Her gaze switched to the window where she saw a large semi backing up to one of the barns. But her mind wasn't on Vicki. "I could always use one of the bunkhouses at my place…"

A scowl crossed Dean's face. "Those aren't livable either, at least, not for a woman. Alfred's living in one because he has to be there on the place, but most guys can rough it for awhile if they have to."

When Dorine remained silent, her downcast expression touched Dean's heart so deeply that he had to sternly take himself in hand to keep from blurting out that *he* would take care of her!

Instead, he said, "That brings me to the second reason I wanted to see you. Since Melody had her baby early, she didn't have a chance to train anybody to take over while she has her maternity leave. You learned quite a bit about this whole system two years ago when we installed it—I'd like you to fill in for her."

She gazed at him, her dark eyes unfathomable. "You're offering me a job?" She turned over the muddled possibilities *that* would bring.

"Yes. Even though we've all been doing a little of it, Melody's computer work is really getting behind," Dean confessed reluctantly, rubbing the back of his neck with one hand—how many times had she seen him do that when he was frustrated? "You know all business transactions for DeFoe Enterprises are handled here now," he waited for her nod, "and Hazel has been promoted to general office manager. She hasn't finished organizing things yet, so we were all at sea when Melody had to leave so quickly. Darrell jumped on it right away," he waved a hand at the cluttered workspace by the computer, "but he *hates* sitting in front of that thing, he'd rather be out rassling calves."

"So you want me to take Melody's place." She sat back, lifting one booted foot to rest on her knee, thoughtfully rubbing her ankle.

"I realize you'll need time to adjust to what's happened...but right now, there's nothing for you to do over at your place—Alfred and the hands are taking care of the outside work like they've always done. Knowing you, you're going to need something to do to keep from getting restless." He sent her an amused look.

Dorine contemplated the stitching on the side of her boot, deep in thought. It surprised her that she could see his point!

He held his breath—*what would be her reaction? At least she didn't jump all over him about trying to run her life!* "I guess I shouldn't be rushing you, and let you enjoy your first week out of school—"

"It's not that...I was... planning..." she glanced up at the pictures on the wall, not quite ready to divulge her secret. Without the ranch house, there would be no "guests."

"Planning...?" He questioned, raising a dark eyebrow.

She shrugged. "Nothing, just thinking out loud."

He watched her eyes, those beautiful deep brown eyes that reminded him of melted chocolate, eyes that a man could drown in. He mentally shook himself. "If you want the job, I'll pay you the same wages as Melody."

Dorine mulled his offer over...she *did* need ready funds...what he said made sense, and suddenly she saw weeks, perhaps months, stretching before her....waiting on the insurance. But work for *him?!!* Therefore, she could hardly believe herself saying, "I'll consider it." *She was out of her mind!* "I have to do *something* while all this insurance stuff gets straightened out."

"You know the saying, 'the mills of the gods grind slowly'," he replied. Leaning back, he eyed her critically. "Take a few days vacation." He hadn't missed the dark smudges under her eyes.

She gave him an uncertain look, now that she'd half-ways committed herself. "If I decide to take this job, I'll start immediately, no reason not to. But first, I have to talk to Alfred and the insurance company, then check on Blaze. We didn't get to rodeo last summer because of that tour I went on with the college choir in Europe... I've really missed the circuit...missed riding in the Badlands too and I'm looking forward to doing that again."

Dean drew in his breath sharply as a frown settled on his brow. "Dorine, the insurance investigator doesn't want anybody poking around there at the ranch except Alfred and the hands—"

Her eyes sparked dangerously. "That is *my* place and I'll go—" she stopped when he held up his hand.

"Yes, it's your place," he replied patiently as though talking to a child, "but if there *are* rustlers, or if there *are* vandals, they might still be around, and it could be dangerous for a woman by herself." He eyed her shrewdly. "I'm sure you know that a couple of guys can overpower *any* woman…unless maybe she's a lady wrestler."

She narrowed her eyes and stared back at him, her chin lifted in a defiant angle. "You mean I can't even check on my own cattle?"

He nodded. "That's just about the size of it, prairie chick…" he gave her a sidelong glance. "Unless someone goes with you…can you give me your promise not to ride alone over there until this whole thing is settled?" His steely voice brooked no nonsense.

For a moment it looked as though she would argue with him, but even as indecision flitted across her face, her chin lifted a little higher, and she gave an abrupt nod, signaling her agreement.

Relief flooded through him. "That's that, then! I've got the name of the insurance guy there in my Rolodex if you want to call him, and until your car is fixed, *if* it is fixable, take my pickup and when you've talked to Alfred, come on back here—you can ask Hazel about the recent upgrades in the computers." The phone rang and he reached for it, signaling their conversation was over as he launched into a business discussion.

*Well, I guess that puts me in my place!* She felt miffed until she remembered that Dean headed up a large organization and his position demanded a lot of him. He'd been blest with a natural ability to lead but he also expected people to recognize that he was in charge. Just now, he'd presented her with a solution to one problem, and assuming it was solved, was moving on with his day…she swallowed her "miff" and went out.

Hazel was delighted that Dorine was considering working in the office, and quickly ran through Melody's workload. Satisfied that she could handle the job if she decided to take it, Dorine excused herself to make a few phone calls before heading for her ranch.

Opening the door of Dean's late-model pickup, she hopped in to slide behind the wheel. The scent of his familiar aftershave lingered in the cab, reminding her of last night when he'd held her in his arms, comforting her after her devastating discovery. Come to think of it, every time she smelled pine scent, she'd thought of him… it hadn't been too hard to control her tongue just now, but—she'd done it! She felt a certain sense of victory and sent an arrow prayer of thanks. But a niggling doubt wiggled in—how long would it last? *Then why consider working for him?!!* said the little voice. "Oh, go away!" Dorine grumbled, reaching for the ignition.

Backing up and turning down the driveway, she drove past the road that led to the ranch housing for the employees, a neat cluster of cottages off to her left. The hottest days of summer had not yet turned the grass dry and brown, but a warm breeze promised to speed up the process. Bed sheets on a clothesline were strung out behind one of the cottages, and a small child was riding a trike in front of another. Lawns were green patches around each little house, and trees had been planted along the driveways. The year-round employees, all of whom she knew, lived right at their job without worrying about driving to work through a Dakota blizzard in the winter. The married men could spend more time with their families.

She thought about the bunkhouses at *her* ranch, how her father had painted and fixed them up, but they wouldn't compare to the cozy cottages Dean provided for his employees—bunkhouses were usually for single men. Thinking of her place reminded her of the conversation she'd just had with the insurance company.

The investigator who was working on her claim, Bryce Martin, was out of the Rapid City office today, but a secretary assured her that he would get her message. The claims department had all the paperwork from Alfred and that was all that was needed at the present time. Dorine had hung up, frustrated, knowing there was nothing more she could do…and that brought her face to face with her immediate future—which included Dean's offer of work. She sighed heavily, knowing already what her answer would have to be.

# CHAPTER FIVE

Dorine dreaded the sight of the yellow barricade tape in front of her house as she drove in the yard. It was quiet like the day before and she wondered where Alfred was. Did he get his own breakfast now that he was here alone? Or did he go into town to Robin's Sweet Schoppe, like some of the bachelor ranchers did?

Pulling up in front of the barn, she determined not to look at the house, and instead, searched the yard and corrals for Alfred. A tractor was just backing out of the machine shed and she recognized her cousin. He saw her coming across the yard, turned off the engine and shifted in his seat as she stopped beside the tractor.

"I see you got home okay," he said gruffly, adjusting his dark sunglasses. As she often had in the past, she wondered again how her mother's brother could produce such a withdrawn, almost sullen son. However, it couldn't have been easy for him to leave his former job and a regular paycheck to move out here five years ago, but he'd never indicated that he regretted the move.

"I drove in about sundown last night."

"That was some mess to walk into," his voice conveyed sympathy. "Where'd ya spend the night, over at DeFoes?"

She nodded. "It *was* quite a shock, seeing the house like that. Dean came over and asked if I wanted to have Darcy's room till we get this mess straightened out." He didn't comment. She continued, "I called the insurance company this morning and they said you've given them all the information they need, and told me in no uncertain terms that I can't live in the house right now...I *hate* being told that I can't do something with my own property!" She kicked a rock with the toe of her boot and watched it roll away.

Alfred gave her a slight grin. "Yeah, I remember." Then he sobered. "I been workin' on the machinery, gettin' ever'thin' ready for hayin'." She couldn't tell if he was looking at her or not, with those dark glasses. He was short-statured, with narrow shoulders and a thin face topped by wire-straight salt and pepper hair. Like most ranchers, he dressed in worn jeans, faded work shirt, boots and a western-styled straw hat.

"Dean also said you guys suspect rustlers?" She squinted up and caught his brusque nod. "How come you never said anything? He's lost stock and said we did too. How many?"

"Not as many as some, but enough," he replied evasively. He named the number and added, "Nothin' we can do anyways, till they catch—whoever it was."

"You still could have told me," she chided as he gave her a wary glance. "We're in this together, Alfred, we both have to know what's going on."

He ducked his head. "Di'n't wanta bother ya, figured I and the boys could handle it till ya got home."

Sighing in exasperation, she changed the subject. "Dean's offered me a job until Melody gets back, so I'll be working over there most of the time. But during roundup, I'll be here as always. For now, I can't help with the haying until evenings and on weekends."

He gave her a startled glance as he took off his glasses to wipe them on his shirttail. "Ya don't havta do that, me 'n the boys have got ever'thin' taken care of," he said quickly. "An if you was to come over here alone…well… those vandals could come back an…well, wouldn't want you gittin' hurt or nothin'." His voice sounded gruff but she heard the underlying concern and softened toward him.

"I know Dean and that insurance guy think they could come back, but I wouldn't think so. Would *you* come back to a place where the police might be waiting? No," she shook her head, "that doesn't sound logical." She straightened up. "Did the vandals, or *whoever* they are, get into the ranch office over at the tack room too?"

He shook his head as he pulled his gloves back on and reached down to push the starter button, tilting his head toward the building in question. "Ever'thin's still in there—nothin' was touched far as I kin tell."

She hesitated. "In the reports you mailed to me, I noticed there was quite a drop in birth of new calves this year?"

He gave a brusque nod and fidgeted with the steering wheel, not looking at her. "Yep, you'll see for yourself when we bring 'em in for brandin'. Course, some of that is because of the missin' cattle." He pushed the starter and the engine caught as the tractor roared into life. "Gotta git to work before it gits too hot." He nodded at her and shifted gears.

Dorine stepped away, watching as he maneuvered the tractor around the shed and down the lane towards the hayfields. What a complex man he was, and yet simple at the same time. One moment she could shake him for his reticence and the next, wanted to hug him for his shy concern.

She was, however, glad that she hadn't told him about her plans for the dude ranch; he didn't seem any too pleased that *she* would be around, let alone anyone else. She had always intended for him and his wife to stay on, and they could easily be a part of her planned endeavor, but she didn't know how Vicki would fit in. And would Alfred be comfortable with strangers coming and going all summer?

Walking back to the pickup, her eyes roamed over the yard... strange, the weeds hadn't been cut around the barn. Alfred had routinely taken care of that, but maybe he just hadn't got around to it yet. Well, *she* could! He was working not too far away, so she wouldn't *really* be breaking her promise not to be here alone...

However, she'd also promised to get started on the backlog of work at Dean's office, so the weeds would have to wait for now.

Getting back into the pickup, she experienced that feeling again, of having Dean's comforting presence surrounding her—why couldn't she get that man out of her mind?! She slammed the door hard and forced herself to more pleasant thoughts.

Where was Blaze? After driving through several gates, she stopped the pickup, grabbed her hat off the seat, got out and scanned the horizon. There was a herd of horses grazing out towards the northwest, and she lifted a hand to shield her eyes from the morning sun. The day was starting to heat up so that not a breath of air stirred, and a few insects in the dry prairie grass jumped out of her way as she walked a little farther. She spotted a reddish glint in the scrub trees.

Putting her fingers to her mouth, she gave a shrill whistle, and was rewarded by an answering whinny.

Blaze came out into the opening, his head held high, ears forward alertly as his nostrils flared. She whistled again and he tossed his head, dancing around before breaking into a gallop that brought him thundering up to her. "Whoa, boy, whoa!" Dorine laughed as she stepped back to avoid getting stepped on, and reached up to pat him on the neck. His winter coat had almost shed, and he was sorely in need of a currycomb. Snorting and snuffling, he poked his nose into her other hand. "Are you glad to see me, boy?" Dorine asked softly. The horse's affection was obvious, and she threw both her arms around his neck. He whinnied and broke away, running in small circles around her, then coming back to nudge her again. "You want to go for a ride, right?!!"

She grasped a handful of his mane and swung herself effortlessly onto his back. He turned and proudly cantered out to the pasture, tossing his head and looking back to get instructions from his mistress. Her clear laughter rang out in the air as she let the breeze flow around her—this was pure heaven, to be out here on her own land again and astride her beloved horse. Putting all her troubled thoughts behind her, she lived for the moment as Blaze broke into a gallop. The landscape gradually changed from rich pastureland to the clay and limestone soil that characterized the Badlands, and she slowed the horse to a walk as she once again took in the beauty of the strange shapes in the low hills, ridges and ravines. Picturesque cliffs were striped with the grayish-white soil of the sandstone, and she peered into the occasional cave, wondering what sort of critter could be found there. Sand and gravel crunched under the horse's feet, the sun beat down on her and as there was no breeze among these small canyons, perspiration trickled down her neck into her shirt. She once again thought about the first miners and hunters who arrived here in the frontier period—there was very little plant life, so farmers, who came later, realized the soil was too poor for raising crops. Her fanciful thoughts as a youngster likened this stark environment to that on the moon. She sighed—how wonderful it would be to return to the innocence of that childhood—

Blaze stopped and pricked his ears forward, bringing her back to the present. Shading her eyes, she scanned the horizon, but didn't see anything unusual. Her heartbeat picked up—had Blaze sensed something or *someone*? "Well, it's time we got back anyway, ole boy," she murmured, schooling her voice to match the reverence in this primeval setting. Blaze flicked his ears backwards to hear her, obediently turning when he felt the slight pressure of her knee. He ambled back along the path and stopped to drink from the river while she laid forward across his neck, listening contentedly to the buzzing and singing of insects along the water's edge. A water skeeter darted unerringly over the top of the slow-moving stream…she didn't want to go back, but the real world called, and she urged Blaze into a trot.

She hated to think of the uncertain days ahead, of having all her plans so drastically changed. She wondered again if her dad would have approved of her plans for the dude ranch—he'd had to change ranching methods too, to fit the shifting economy since his grandfather had homesteaded here.

There was nothing here when her great-great-grandparents had arrived—no house, no roads, few neighbors. Yet the Andrews' had stayed, stuck it out and built this ranch into what it was today. It was overwhelming to think that all this had come to her—she was the last of the line.

Did she have the same gumption her ancestors had? Her dad had often said she resembled her grandmother in so many ways, and now she hoped that she had the stamina to keep on like Grandma Andrews had…but it felt so lonely to be the only one.

She reached the pickup and reluctantly slid off the horse. He snuffled and shoved his nose into her hand. "I'll be back," she promised, gazing up at her special friend. He followed her to the pickup and when she got in and closed the door, he tried to put his head in the open window. "Oh, you silly animal! There's no room in here for you!" she laughed, but was deeply touched by the horse's attachment to her.

Blaze followed her to the gate, and after driving through, she had to shoo him away so she could close it. He looked at her expectantly, and her heart turned over. "I know, big boy, I don't want to leave you either," she said softly, giving him one last pat on the nose. He stood gazing after her as she drove back to the barn, and her heart felt a pang at his longing look.

Returning to the DeFoe ranch, she parked in the shade of the cottonwoods and walked briskly to the office. Her spirits had been lifted, and she felt ready to tackle the job Dean was offering.

"Boy, am I glad for air-conditioning! I think I got spoiled at college," she smiled at the women in the office as she headed for the restroom to splash water on her face and tuck a few strands of her hair back into her braid. She returned and slipped into the chair at Melody's workstation.

Glancing at Dean's door, Loretta said, "When we have time, you'll have to tell us about college life."

Darlene grinned. "Yeah, like all the handsome hunks!"

Dorine raised an eyebrow. "There's nothing wrong with the one *you* married!" Darlene nodded and had the grace to blush. Her husband *had* been one of the "hunks" while in school.

"Did you find anybody who swept you off your feet?" Loretta asked dreamily, leaning her elbow on the desk and resting her chin in her hand.

"I was too busy studying, and with my part-time job, there wasn't much time for dating…but there *were* some guys…" Dorine let her voice trail off as she turned on her computer. Then she glanced impishly at the other women. They didn't need to know that the few men she dated had been Christians with the same moral values as she, and their relationships had never progressed beyond holding hands at the movies or on walks around the campus.

Hazel got up to pull out a file drawer. "There's nothing wrong with the young men around here, Loretta," she raised her eyebrow as she glanced at Loretta and shoved papers into a file. "Dorine was right to come home to find her 'hunk', as you put it. Didn't you two do pretty well for yourselves with the local 'hunks'?"

"Oh, we're not complaining, Hazel," Loretta grinned, "but it's so romantic to hear about someone else's love life!"

Dorine laughed and turned her attention to her work. She couldn't imagine marrying any of the young men she'd grown up with around Silverdale, they were too much like brothers and all she could feel for them was a fond affection.

She was unaware that Dean had watched her unobtrusively from his office. His heart swelled at seeing her lively expressions as she talked—she was one gutsy woman, considering what she'd found at her home yesterday. But she was a strong ranch woman, used to a hard life—a life of uncertainties. His heart was full of gratitude that the college environment and overseas travel had not changed her, she was still seemingly content with the simple lifestyle of a rancher. He yearned to have her direct one of her enchanting smiles at him, but he knew he'd have to give her time to realize their changing roles. For now, he was content that she was safe here with him—safe from whatever danger hovered over her ranch.

Some time later, he came out of his office and stopped by her desk. "How's it going?" The sound of his voice caused those crazy flutterings in her stomach again. If she didn't know better, she'd almost believe he'd deliberately lowered his voice to sound soft and seductive—*teasing again!*

Without looking up, she replied, "I'm getting the hang of it—I've only had to interrupt Hazel a couple of times for help." She took a deep breath to steady her jumping heart, and got a whiff of his cologne—*did he need to stand so close?*

"Good. By the way, did you talk to Alfred?"

"Yes, but he seemed…I don't know…kind of edgy, I guess…" This subject was safe territory. She turned and glanced up at him. "I went for a short ride on Blaze—he sure didn't want me to leave, I felt kind of mean driving away, him looking after me over the gate."

A speculative gleam came into Dean's eyes. "Ah-h, what do you think of bringing him over here?"

She tried to hide the pleasure his question brought, answering non-chalantly, "That… seems like a lot of trouble, for just the little while that I'll be here."

Dean resisted the temptation to say that he didn't *ever* want her to leave, aware of the other three women nearby. Instead, he sighed patiently. "Dorine, it might be some time before the insurance company says you can move back in. If you brought Blaze over here, you could see him anytime—he'd settle in real quick once he realizes you're here too."

His logical argument swayed her. She was so used to him *commanding* her to do things, that when he used this calm tactic, she was completed caught off guard. "All right…but I'll pay for his keep—"

This time, Dean couldn't control his irritation. He leaned forward, placing one hand flat on her desk, his nose almost touching hers. In a fierce whisper he said, "You'll do no such thing! Why do you always have to be so obstinate when people want to help you?!"

Struggling with her temper, the remembrance of her promise to God kept her tongue still. Plus, the two younger secretaries were casting curious glances their way. It went against her grain to back down, but she managed to reply quietly, "All right, whatever works."

Dean straightened, a triumphant gleam in his eyes. He looked as though he wanted to say more, hesitated for a moment, then turned away, speaking to Hazel.

Dorine returned her attention to the computer screen but it took some time for her temper to cool.—*why did she let him rattle her cage this way?!!*

Deep in concentration later, she noticed a movement out of the corner of her eye.

Darrell rested his hip against her desk. "Gosh, it's good to have you home! Sorry I couldn't be at your graduation, but you know how the rodeo schedule is—there was a bull with my name on him!" Mischief danced in blue eyes as he crossed his arms over his chest and grinned at her. He smelled of fresh air, sunshine and fragrant hayfields. He was lean and lanky, with a casual, devil-take-the-hindmost approach to life that seemed to attract all sorts of feminine attention. And all *she* could feel for him was a fond affection—they had been comrades in crime ever since she could toddle after him. As youngsters, their mission was to get into as much trouble as possible. Piercing blue eyes, so like his mother's and Dean's, were filled with good humor at the moment. "Wanna go for a ride?"

She was tempted but glanced at the computer screen and the stacks of files waiting for her. "I'd really love to, but I've got all this to do. By the way, Dean has offered to let me bring Blaze over here."

He nodded. "Good idea!...I'm really sorry about what happened over at your place." His demeanor changed as he frowned.

"Do you know much about it?" she asked as she punched a button to save files.

"No, probably not much more than you already know," he replied softly, lowering his voice. "I really like having you here, but it's a bummer you can't even live in your own house...not that it would be pleasant anyway, with Vicki...." his voice trailed away. "I guess I shouldn't say anything, but she's such a snob! I can't imagine how you've gotten along with her all these years."

"You know she's a city girl, Darrell, and it's been hard on her to live so far out here away from everything." Dorine's naturally compassionate personality chose to defend her cousin's wife.

"Yeah, but she shouldn't act like we're a bunch of ignoramuses, either! I didn't sweat my brains out for that college degree for nothing, but she acts like we're beneath her."

"She needs to know the love of the Lord," Dorine said softly. "I've tried to witness to her, but she coldly says that when she needs religion, *she'll* go to church."

"Kind of like somebody else we know," Darrell replied quietly, glancing at Dean's office door.

A sadness crossed Dorine's face as she glanced at the door too. "He still won't listen, will he?"

"It's hard to believe that he was once so active in church." Darrell looked down at his dusty boots and shook his head. "When he began missing services after Dad died, it really bothered me. After *your* dad died, he quit going altogether. He's used to everything always going his way, and those were circumstances he couldn't control."

"Does... he have a girlfriend?" Dorine asked casually as she pretended to look through a file folder.

"Oh, he dates occasionally. Right now, there's a redhead over in Rapid City, but he's not serious about her—"

"—How do you know that?" she interrupted. Her heart plummeted, but she brought herself up short—why should *she* care?!!

Darrell gave a short bark of laughter. "Oh, little cowgirl, us guys know! Believe me, we know!" He stood up. "By the way, are you going to rodeo this summer?" He'd always been one of her encouragers and they'd often team-roped together.

"I don't really know, I haven't thought of it since I'm home—as soon as they'll let me move back into my house, there'll be tons of work waiting for me...there may not be time to rodeo." If he only knew how much she missed being on the circuit, traveling to events with the two brothers as they'd done for over six summers.

"Think about it," he stretched his arms above his head, "I guess if you won't go riding with me, I'll have to find somebody else—" he broke off and turned to Hazel, who was just putting down the phone. "You want to go for a ride with me?" He batted his eyelashes, glancing at the other women, who giggled at his outrageous teasing.

Hazel grinned saucily. "Oh, yes, and what would you do for the poor sway-backed horse after I got off him? Go on with you, I've got work to do!" Her bubbly laughter followed him out the door.

"That boy," Hazel shook her head as she peered at her computer screen. "It's too bad he can't convince Sharry to marry him."

Loretta laughed softly. "That will take some doing, knowing the way she feels about rodeo cowboys!" She punched the print button.

Darlene agreed as her fingers clacked across the computer keys. "Everybody can see they love each other, but they don't have brains enough to do something about it."

Dorine laughed, turning back to her own computer. Sharry Schafer and Darrell had been "The Twosome" in high school. She was a petite, bubbly blonde, popular with everyone and a top student. But the relationship had been peppered with so many breakups and reunions it was like a soap opera. Sharry moved to Rapid City after nursing school and worked in one of the big hospitals there. It was quite a drive from Silverdale, but Darrell still made the trip occasionally; however, he never spoke of the little blonde and Dorine sensed she'd be trespassing on private ground if she asked. She couldn't figure out what was the matter with them, it was so obvious they were meant for one another.

Dorine paused, gazing sightlessly at the computer screen. For the hundredth time, she wondered why she had never felt that way about anyone. She couldn't envision *any* of her high school classmates in a romantic way—she could ride and rope with the best of them. She thought of the love her parents had—their love for each other but more importantly, love for Christ—that had been the glue that held them together. Her dad had been a one-woman man—to him, Amy was the "A" in the Circle A brand, and after she was gone, he concentrated on his daughter, never even considering dating again. Would she be like him? Once she found her life mate, would she never look at anyone else?

Some time later, Dean came out of his office, settling his hat on his head. He came up behind her and put his hands on her shoulders as he leaned down to peer at the screen. His casual touch caused her heart to speed up until she realized he was only studying information on the screen. Hoping he wouldn't notice, she tried to edge unobtrusively away.

"Say, that's a good idea!" he complimented her. Pointing at the screen, he continued, "I would never have thought of setting that up like that—" he glanced down at her, approval in his blue eyes. He squeezed her shoulder lightly, then astonished her by tapping the end of her nose with his finger! "Good job!" He stepped away, and her skin felt cold where his warm fingers had rested.

Swallowing hard, she tried not to let him see how much his touch affected her. "Be careful with your compliments, DeFoe, you may have to widen the doors to accommodate my big head!" She glanced impishly at Loretta, who stifled a giggle.

He smiled mysteriously before turning to leave. Loretta and Darlene both glanced at the door closing behind him, then back at Dorine. "Boy, you can get away with anything, can't you? As good a boss as he is, I'd be afraid to say something like that to him," Darlene commented.

Dorine felt heat rise in her cheeks. "He's got it into his head that I need an older brother."

"Yeah, sure, *brother*!" quipped Lorraine, chuckling knowingly.

"Is that why you two always argue?" Darlene asked innocently.

"We don't argue!" Dorine replied, turning to her computer. "We just have…vigorous discussions!" Laughter followed her comment.

# CHAPTER SIX

"Ready for dinner?" Dean's deep voice interrupted her.

Dorine's stomach fluttered. It must be hunger pains. She glanced at the wall clock to see it was already noon. "I have to finish this entry." He nodded, waiting, having no idea that she was so aware of him she heard every rustle when he moved.

He talked easily on the walk to the house. Dorine, on the other hand, felt almost tongue-tied and took care not to brush against his arm. He asked questions about the accounts she'd worked on, and she was pleased that she could give knowledgeable answers. Then he asked, "What was Alfred doing when you got over there?"

She repeated the conversation she'd had with her cousin, but noticed Dean's preoccupation, which was confirmed when he asked, "Did you notice anything different—you mentioned he seemed edgy?" He stopped, searching her face, one hand resting on his hip.

She gazed back, trying to guess his motive for asking. "Is there something you haven't told me?" It was hard to guess what he was thinking behind those inquisitive eyes. *Those beautiful blue eyes...*

Dean glanced behind him, then stepped back a few feet to lean against the fender of his pickup, parked at the edge of the lawn near the house. "We-l-l," he squinted at her, "I don't have anything concrete to go on, but Bryce and I suspect...well, that he may be involved in this whole mess."

Dorine's quickly indrawn breath came out in a question. "Why? What makes you think so?" She focused on his lips, and realized what beautiful straight white teeth he had...*this was crazy!*

Dean shifted his weight, crossed his arms and looked down at his legs, crossed at the ankles. "He acts like he doesn't want anyone around the place, and doesn't venture any ideas about what's been going on." He held up his hand at her impatient noise as he glanced at her. "I know, I know, he doesn't talk much at any time, but this is different..." He gazed off into the distance. "I can't put my finger on it, and neither can Bryce, it's just a feeling we have."

Dorine digested this news, then slowly said, "I wanted to look at the books but I can do that later…he said they were still in the tackroom/office—thankfully they weren't in the house. But if the calf crop is as poor as he says, there won't be much bookkeeping to do anyway."

"What do you mean, a poor calf crop?" Dean inquired carefully. "When I flew over your herd earlier this spring, I estimated the new calves at about 90 percent—that's pretty good."

She squinted up at him, and answered slowly, "Alfred sent the latest reports last month and said he was roughly guessing we had only about two-thirds of what we did last year."

Dean shook his head. "That's what I mean, Dorine, something just doesn't add up." He lifted his hand to wave as an employee drove by.

"But nothing has ever been amiss that I can see…" Her bewilderment tugged at his heart.

"Just another piece of the puzzle, prairie chick." He reached out to touch her shoulder. "Promise me something, will you?" He waited for her slow nod. "Don't say anything to him about this conversation, okay?" She looked puzzled. "If what we suspect is true, it might tip him off—if it's not true, he'll never know—and we can all avoid an embarrassing situation."

Dorine was confused. Why would her cousin want to cheat or rob her, *or* himself? The ranch was as much his livelihood as hers.

"Well, no use trying to figure anything out on an empty stomach—let's go eat!" Dean indicated she should precede him up the walk, opening the screen door for her. As she passed in front of him, she caught a whiff of that pleasant pine, reminding her of the forests in the Black Hills. This sudden awareness of him was really unnerving! Thankfully he seemed oblivious of her musings as he entered the sunporch behind her, taking off his old straw cowboy hat and hanging it on a peg before turning left into the combination washroom/bathroom.

Dorine continued on into the house, her nose appreciating the dinner aromas from the food being put on the table. Marci turned from slicing the homemade bread and carried a plate of the fragrant, just-out-of-the-oven slices to the table, then she filled a pitcher of ice cubes with water and set it on the table. "Sit down, dear, and we'll get the food on while you read your mail," she said as she handed Dorine a handful of letters. Dorine raised a puzzled gaze and Marci smiled. "Dean got your letters from the mailman, along with ours."

Luckily, she'd turned away because Dorine did a slow burn—*who did he think he was?!!* Mrs. Mac ambled to the table with a large platter of fried chicken to join the mashed potatoes, gravy and creamed peas already there. Dorine damped down her irritation and opened cards from family friends, congratulating her on her graduation, and a few contained welcome checks.

The screendoor slammed and Dean and Darrell's voices could be heard discussing the morning's events as they washed up.

Coming into the kitchen, they seated themselves as Dorine, Mrs. Mac and Marci took their places. Dean raised his eyebrows at Dorine's glare and gave her an innocent look as Darrell bowed his head to give thanks. Dorine lowered her eyes, but chanced a peek at Dean. His hands were on the table, knife and fork in hand, his eyes staring at the butter plate, with no semblance of prayer. She supposed his only concession to the Lord was to at least be quiet, and he probably did *that* for his mother's sake. The irritation died away and her heart constricted as she closed her eyes. *Oh, Lord, open his eyes, let him see You!*

They began dishing up, the aromatic food scents mingling with cooling air from the slowly turning overhead fan. Conversation moved easily to the weather, cattle prices, upcoming rodeos and community events. Dorine looked around the table at the familiar faces of all these dear people—yes, even Dean—suddenly realizing she felt at home, at ease, contentment—it was as though the last few years away at college had never happened. She was here with neighbors who were more like family, enjoying a dinner like she'd shared countless times before—but now, as an adult, she realized how much their support meant to her.

"What's the matter, dear? Is something wrong?" Marci asked

with concern as she passed the gravy to Mrs. Mac.

"No, no...everything's fine...just fine," Dorine replied contentedly.

Dean didn't miss the parade of emotions that had just fluttered over her face and since he could always read her like a book, he dropped his gaze and hid a smile behind his coffee cup—he'd made it to first base—in spite of that glare that could have curdled the gravy!

After stuffing themselves on apple pie dripping with brown sugar and whipped cream, they carried their plates to the kitchen counter. The men went into the living room to watch the noon cattle report on television, while the women finished clearing away the meal. Then Dorine took the hall phone with the long cord and sat on the bottom step of the stairs as she dialed the Sweet Schoppe. At the sound of Robin's voice, she caroled "Hi-i-i! I'm home!"

"Dorine!" squealed her friend. "I heard you got in yesterday, but I guess you were so shook up about the house that you forgot to call."

"You don't even seem interested in where I am!"

"Well, you're naturally at DeFoes!"

"Why naturally?" Dorine questioned, a frown furrowing her brow.

"Because...well, Marci said you'd be staying there until the insurance company settles the claim."

"You mean *Dean* said I'd be staying." She kept her voice low.

"Oh, what difference does it make? You're here now and home to stay! When can you come over?"

Dorine accepted the change of subject. "As soon as I can get off work."

"Work?" squeaked Robin. "You've got a job? *Where*?!!" Dorine laughed and told her, then carefully asked, "Did Dean tell you not to let me know about the house?"

There was a hesitation. "Yes, and I'm sorry about that, Dorine. I really thought you had a right to know, but..."

There was amusement in Dorine's voice. "What did he do, *threaten* you?"

"No!" quickly replied her friend. "You know he'd never do that! But...well, he's already offered me the contract for the food concession when he opens the arena, and even though I know he'd never go back on his word, I just didn't want to do anything to create an awkward situation."

Dorine didn't blame her. Business had slacked off at the Sweet Schoppe since the new station and deli had opened at the freeway exit, and any new business for her might mean the difference between Robin staying open or closing her little café.

Dorine laughed softly. "You don't need to explain, I understand... how are the boys?"

She listened distractedly as Dean came out of the living room and walked through the kitchen on his way back to work. Her heart picked up extra beats as she admired his relaxed, familiar gait.

"Earth to Dorine."

"I'm here," Dorine replied. Why did she feel this strangeness all of a sudden whenever Dean came near? She'd grown up seeing him in his everyday work clothes, why did they suddenly seem so...so *attractive* on his lean, athletic body?

"Did a good-lookin' guy walk by? Which reminds me, you ought to see that insurance guy, Bryce Martin—what a hunk!"

"You're supposed to be married!" Dorine protested.

"That doesn't mean I'm blind!" quipped Robin. "Is he there?"

"No, I haven't met him yet."

"Boy, get ready to hold on to your socks!"

"You've got me curious now, I can hardly wait to meet him."

"Well, I gotta go," said Robin. "Are you coming in later?"

"I'll see," murmured Dorine. She hung up the phone and hurried back over to the office, wondering why her hands felt clammy and her heart still hadn't returned to normal. *Darn that Dean!*

A welcome call to her desk a little later was from Pastor Rick. "I'm thankful that our prayers have brought you home safely—I've doubled my praying for you this past month, after we heard about the vandalism." Buster, the ranch foreman, came out of Dean's office, saw her looking his way, grinned and gave her a two-fingered salute before his lanky strides carried him out the door. Dorine watched him leave. *Why didn't her heart flutter over him?* He was tall, lanky and handsome too! But she'd also known him all her life...

"Thank you, Pastor. It seems everyone knew about the vandalism except me—the vandalized!" she said lightly.

"Yes, well, Mrs. DeFoe and her family thought you would try to come home right away, and so close to graduation, she was afraid you wouldn't get to take your finals," he replied. "Have you heard anything new about the investigation?" *Mrs. DeFoe and her family?—try plain ole Dean!* After filling him in on details and promising a solo for Sunday morning worship, she hung up.

Dean came out of his office to talk to Hazel several times. "Oh, and you probably better order more ammunition, we're almost out." Dorine looked over her shoulder at him, enjoying the deep timber of his voice, and how smoothly he gave instructions—*why didn't he talk that way to her instead of always demanding she do what he wanted!!* He turned, caught her watching him and audaciously gave her a wink before going back into his office! *Had his eyelashes always been so long?* She shook her head—this was *Dean*, the master manipulator!!

She had to concentrate on something else—like, if her own ranch hands had their supplies for the coming roundup. She herself had handled guns since she took a course in safety in her early teens but her dad had taught her to shoot when she was 12—he cautioned it was for protection against poisonous snakes, not ever for anything else.

Her thoughts were interrupted by Dean calling her into his office. At the sight of that wavy black curl falling over his forehead, she took a deep breath to calm her annoyingly fast heartbeat.

Not looking up from the cluttered desk, he said, "I'd like you to sit in on some up-coming meetings this week and next, along with Hazel. I want you to get an idea of the plans we're discussing. Darrell and Mom will be here too. Darcy and Joe will listen on concall."

His terse instructions jerked her back to reality. "Dean." She spoke firmly. "I'm not going to keep on working for you, remember,

I have my own place to run?" She planted herself in front of his desk.

He dropped his pen, no, he half-ways *threw* down his pen, leaned back in his chair and gave her a sharp glare, the blue of his eyes turning icy. "And just why are you still dwelling on that?" Gone was the earlier pleasant companion, and Dean, the antagonist, was back! "I've told you what the insurance company said."

She waved her hand in the air. "I meant *after* they're done!"

He straightened slowly and fixed his gaze on her face. "We don't know when that will be, do we?" he replied with false sweetness.

"Well, I *do* have plans—" suddenly aware their conversation might be overheard in the outer office, she stepped back and closed the door before turning around to face him, her anger building.

"What kind of plans?" he barked, a frown creasing his forehead. "Alfred and the hands can keep on running the place just as they have the past four years, and with your job here, you don't have time to go running over there whenever the mood strikes you!"

She leaned slightly forward, enunciating her words as though to a particularly dense person. "Listen up, DeFoe, I'm not going to keep on working for you—I'm going to have a guest ranch, and I'll need time to get it up and running." She hadn't meant to divulge her secret in quite this manner but now it was out—and he didn't like it!

"*What*?!!" he bellowed, rocking forward in his chair. It squealed in protest at the quick movement. "You don't have the *slightest* idea what you're talking about! Do you have any idea of what it's going to cost to fix that place up? Even if the insurance company pays for the damages, you'd still have to put out a lot of money to get started!" She couldn't remember his eyes ever being so angry.

At each of his discouraging remarks, she blinked—then began to see red. The more he talked, the further up her chin tilted. Forgotten was her promise to be tactful and kind.

Finally, she leaned over and slapped her hands on his desk. "Now you listen here!" she began in a deadly quiet voice. "I've been studying all this out for almost two years—I didn't just start thinking about it yesterday—" she stopped for an angry breath— "I know *exactly* how much it's going to cost! Do you really think I'm so ignorant and unprepared to go into this with my eyes shut?!! I've done plenty of research, and," she brought her face close to his, "if *someone* had told me about the vandalism, I could have been taking *that* into consideration too!"

At the beginning of her tirade, Dean's face had darkened even more, but as Dorine's voice got louder and began to quaver, he mentally backed down. *What had he started? He was beginning to wish he'd kept his mouth shut!*

But she wasn't done yet. "You think you know everything!—"

"Now Dorine—"

"Well, you don't! You haven't the slightest idea of what's best for me, so I'm telling you to butt out!" To her everlasting embarrassment, Dorine felt tears coming. "And another thing—when are you going to get that squeaky chair fixed?!!" She ignored his out-stretched hand and turned on her heel towards the door.

"Dorine, wait—" His words were cut off by the sharp crack of the slammed door. He sat stunned at the whirlwind that had just blown out of his office. Should he let her go, or chase after her? Undecided for a moment, he puffed out an exasperated sigh before lunging to his feet.

The secretaries looked up in surprise as Dorine hurried by them. "I'll be back later." Hazel frowned, glancing at the other two women who looked stunned as Dorine pushed through the outer doors.

For a moment, there was complete silence, then Dean's door was yanked open and he hurried out, taking long strides through the office. Hazel stared after him. "Well, I never—!" She glanced at Loretta and Darlene. "I don't suppose I have to tell you that things that happen here, stay here." Both women nodded and exchanged uneasy glances.

Dorine rushed across the yard toward the house, blindly running, not knowing where she was headed and not caring, when she crashed into a solid body.

"Whoa!" Darrell grabbed her by the upper arms. "What's wrong? Why are you crying? What happened?" She shook her head, covering her face with her hands, not wanting him to see her so unglued. "Is somebody hurt?" She shook her head again. "Come on, let's go over here and sit down," Darrell put his arm around her and guided her towards a grouping of chairs on the lawn under the cottonwoods. He looked up at the sound of hurried footsteps and saw his brother coming. "What's wrong? What happened?"

"Nothing!" Dean snapped, brushing by him.

"Whaddaya mean, 'nothing'? What's she crying for?"

Halting next to Dorine, Dean shot a piercing glare at his brother. "It's got nothing to do with you! Go away and leave us alone!"

Darrell stared at him, glanced at Dorine, then shrugged his shoulders. "If you say so..." He turned, heading to the barn, shaking his head. What was going on with those two? They scrapped like two mad cats tied together in a bag, or like high schoolers in the throes of puppy love—he stopped abruptly, considering that thought, turning slowly to stare at the couple under the trees.

He began grinning as he resumed walking, and by the time he got to the barn, he was whistling.

Dorine leaned against a tree, trying to stifle the tears. The waxy leaves of the cottonwood rattled together above her in a puff of breeze as she loudly sniffed. *Where was that tissue? Why didn't she ever have a tissue when she needed one?!!*

"Dorine?...look, I didn't mean to upset you," Dean stood helplessly behind her, curling and uncurling his clenched fists. Why did things always have to become so emotional where she was concerned?!!

No response. The quietness was broken only by birdsong overhead. The sun's intense heat seemed to suck the very air out of one's lungs, not helping this situation. "Look, I didn't mean to jump all over you like that. It's just that...well, it took me by surprise. You've never said *anything* about running a...a guest ranch." He made it sound like a dirty word.

No response. A soft breeze stole over the lawn, gently moving the stray wispy hair around Dorine's face. Dean raised his hand to brush it back, wavered a moment, then let his hand fall. "Dorine? Please look at me." The breeze created a small dust whirl, dancing on by.

She sniffed and pulled herself up straight. *How could she have yelled at him like that—was that showing him God's love? What was the matter with her?* Not only that, but he was her employer now, and he would be within his rights to fire her for her outburst. A wave of embarrassment swept over her as she thought about the three women in the office who had no doubt overheard them. She ventured a glance up at him as she wiped the last of her tears away with the back of her hand. He was staring at her with a perplexed look so unlike him that it caused a snag in her breathing.

"I'm sorry, Dean," she whispered, gazing down at her fingers, nervously twisting them together. "I had no right to explode at you like that. I'm sorry. If you'd rather I don't work for you, I'll understand."

One of the ranch hands drove by and puffs of dust settled back to the heated ground.

Dean sighed, running his hand through his hair as he looked down at the parched ground. "Yes, I want you working for me. But what I *don't* like, is us at each other's throats all the time." He turned troubled eyes on her. "Not only because it's bad for office morale, but… I thought we were friends, that we could talk to each other about anything. Instead…we just… argue."

She nodded, her eyes downcast. "It's my fault, not yours. I'm sorry." She had composed herself and really was remorseful.

"Oh for cryin' out loud, will you quit apologizing?!!"

"Are we arguing again?" she asked softly, a slight twitch to her lips.

When she dared a peek up at him with a mischievous look in those dark eyes, he felt a lurch of his heart and the anger ebbed away. Her crazy sense of humor popped up at the darndest times, completely defusing his temper and he wanted to hug her!

"No, we're not arguing," he replied softly, reaching out to run the back of his fingers down her cheek. "And what does my squeaky chair have to do with anything?" His voice was deeper, softer.

His touch was almost her undoing—never had she felt such a reaction to another man's touch and she couldn't look at him. "It's been squeaky ever since I can remember...and it finally got to me..."

He gazed down at her. "Look, you don't have to come back to the office right now." He glanced back. "I imagine it might be kind of..."

"...embarrassing," she finished for him, nodding, still not looking at him as she tucked her fingers in her front pockets. "In fact, a whole lot embarrassing...I'm sor—"

"Don't you dare say it!"

She tried to hide her grin by ducking her head but he took her chin in his hand and tipped her head up. *What am I gonna do with you?* Out loud, he said, "I'm the one who should be apologizing. If you want to talk about this guest ranch you're planning, I'm all ears. In fact, I'd like you to bounce your ideas off me...like you used to."

Her grin faded and she turned her head away. "Not...not right now." Her heart sorrowed for the rapport they used to have.

His hand dropped to his side and he made a decision. "You haven't even seen any of your friends yet, Dorine. You don't need to dive into work right away. Why don't you take my pickup into town to see Robin. She's expecting you, isn't she?" Knowing how close the two women had been all their lives, he knew Dorine needed that feminine comfort, someone her own age to confide in—he felt a slight jab in his heart that she didn't trust him enough to let him be that one.

She shook her head. "I've barely made a dent in those files."

"They've laid there this long, they can lay there another day."

"I...I would like to see her," she answered shyly.

"The keys are in the pickup...stay as long as you like. I'll tell Mom and Mrs. Mac." He turned and retraced his steps to the office. She watched him walk away, and felt that stirring again in the vicinity of her heart. He was so willing for things to be right between them...and he *was* kind. *Heavenly Father, it seems that's all I'm doing, is asking You to help me to control my wayward tongue,"* she prayed in desperation. *"I'll never convince him of Your unconditional love if I can't control my temper and stop my hurtful words. He was once so faithful to You, help him to find the way back. If I can be used in this purpose, give me the grace and the patience. Amen."*

# CHAPTER SEVEN

By the time she slid behind the wheel, she had a new determination and a firmer grip on her emotions. Glancing at her watch, she saw it would be the ideal time to catch Robin at her least-busy time, the lull between dinner and supper at the Sweet Schoppe. She smiled as she remembered that in college, "dinner" had meant the evening meal, not noon like here in ranch country.

Noticing dark thunderheads building in the western sky, she thought how appropriate—Dean's thunder and her lightning tongue! Only with God's help and her vigilance over her tongue, would things ever improve. The wailing notes of a forlorn western song came over the radio, mirroring her feelings as she drove to town.

Parking near Silverdale's popular little café, Dorine pocketed the keys and walked into the Sweet Schoppe, where barely-audible western music created a soft background. Just stepping through the door brought a soothing calm to her spirit—the decor had never changed since she had come here with her parents as a small child; years later, it was the "in" place for her high school crowd. The long, spacious room had a lengthy glassed-in candy/bakery counter stretching along the wall to her left, booths were to the right, cloth-covered tables in the middle. At the back, a high counter and stools divided the main room from the kitchen passthrough. Robin looked up when the door opened, her eyes lighting up when she saw her best friend. Hurrying out to Dorine, she enveloped her in a tight hug, then stood back, running her eyes up and down Dorine's slender figure. "You look great!"

"And you've got flour on your nose, as usual!" laughed Dorine, already feeling better. Robin was as plump as she was in high school, and having two children hadn't helped her weight. A riot of curly dark red hair covered her head, and freckles marched over her impish nose, while hazel eyes twinkled merrily up at her friend.

"Come on, sit down, we've got gobs to catch up on! How was your trip home? Did you have any trouble? And how come you didn't call me right away?!!"

Dorine shook her head as she sank down on a red, vinyl-covered chair. "Whoa! Fine, yes, and I was so upset about finding my house like that, that my brain just shut down."

"What do you mean, you had trouble?" Dorine felt a tug on her heart for this dear friend that understood her so well she could zero in on the fact that she'd had car trouble. After relating the details, she finished by saying, "Now the car won't start at all."

Robin raised an eyebrow. "When are you going to get rid of that old clunker? I worry about you driving around in it." The phone rang and she bustled over to find a bakery customer. "Anyway, how is it to work for Dean?" She came back and settled down in the chair opposite Dorine.

Dorine looked fondly at this life-long friend of hers. Her infectious laughter and lovable personality endeared her to everyone in town. She and Randy, a long-haul trucker, were married a week after graduation from high school and Dorine teased Robin that Randy must have been home at least twice in the last few years—they had two children!

Dorine shrugged. "Okay, I guess…"

"Just 'okay'?!!" Robin hooted. "Don't tell me you're still scrapping?"

Dorine smiled wryly and looked towards the window. "We just got into it a little while ago—"

"And?"

"I didn't tell him about my plans to start a guest ranch, and he hit the ceiling—"

"You didn't tell me, *either!* How come?!!" Robin's voice rose in disbelief.

"I wanted to see if it was feasible first, before I said anything to *anybody*."

"Hel-lo!" Robin sang out, "this is me, remember, good ole Robin?"

"I know," Dorine looked sheepish. "But you've got your hands full here, with your family and running a business—"

"Never too busy for you, Dorine!" Robin stated emphatically, laying a plump hand on Dorine's arm. The touch was comforting.

Dorine sighed and looked down. "I know. I probably I should have told you, but Dean has a way of finding things out, and I just didn't want him exploding all over me about it."

"Which he did anyway, right? So what did you gain?" scolded her friend. "Besides, why is it so important whether he knows or not, you don't have to answer to him...do you?" she asked slyly.

"No!"

"Dorine, you may think I'm out of line to say this, but Dean cares a lot more about you than you imagine, and *I think*," she pointed at herself, "that you've got feelings for him, whether you *admit* it or not."

Dorine sat up straight and stared at her. "What's this? Are you the same Robin who once said we should stake him out on an ant hill and pour honey on him?!!"

Robin blushed in remembrance but her face softened. "I *used* to feel that way about him because I could see how he upset you...but kiddo," she leaned forward and put her hand over Dorine's, "you're both adults now, and it's time to put those kind of feelings away, just like it says in the Bible."

Trust her old friend to be blunt. "I know you're right...but...he just irritates me so much! Always bossing me around—"

"Have you ever thought that it's *because* he cares so much, that's why he appears to be bossing you?"

"Well don't tell me that Randy does that to you!"

Robin's eyes softened and a beautiful smile lit her face. "No, but our circumstances are different. He's always treated me like a porcelain doll—" her eyes twinkled— "when I'm really more like an over-stuffed one!" Her laughter was contagious and Dorine giggled.

She could see the love that Robin and Randy shared, and a stab of envy went through her. She'd always thought that she would marry someday and have children, but so far, Mr. Right had not presented himself. She knew she had plenty of time, but now that she'd achieved her goal of a college education, she wanted to hurry on with the next phase, which meant the guest ranch. After that...*then what?* said that irritating little voice.

Dorine sobered. "Dean would rather *die* than treat me like I was made of porcelain—and I wouldn't want him to. Besides, a woman rancher can't be delicate, she'd never last."

"But her man can still treat her that way...if she lets him..."

Dorine sighed and looked down at her fingers. "After this morning, he'd laugh if he thought I wanted him to treat me that way—I let him have it with both barrels, but," she added sadly, "I'm not proud of it— God can't use me to show His love if I can't even keep a civil tongue in my head. I'm going to have to turn over a new leaf and control this impulsive tongue of mine," she finished wryly.

Robin's merry laugh spilled out of her. "*That* will be the day! You might as well wear a sign on your mouth that says 'Remove left foot and insert right'!" Then she sobered and leaned towards Dorine. "But why don't you try this on for size—what if his so-called bossiness is his way of showing you how *much* he cares about you?" Dorine snorted. "I'm serious— do you remember actually when he started 'bossing' you? It was right after your dad died. You were alone all of a sudden, no father, no brother, no close male relative— Dean was trying to show you that he was there for you and that you could turn to him."

Dorine searched her eyes as she spoke, and a doubt was planted. She'd always known of Dean's protectiveness— how he cared for his mother, how he and Darrell kept an eye out for each other on rodeo days, how he expected his ranch hands to put their families first. In her stubborn bid for independence, had she misjudged his motives? Indecision flickered through her eyes.

Robin concluded her case. "Do you recall ever scrapping this much with anyone else? No? Maybe it's because you never cared enough about anyone else..."

Dorine scowled. "All Dean has ever done is make me want to spit nails!...but no more," her face cleared. "You're going to really have to pray for the 'new me'!" she emphasized.

The bell over the door tinkled and Robin glanced at the clock before getting up. "Well, duty calls...and I'll be praying for you and this situation, Dorrie." The familiar nick-name caused a lump in Dorine's throat and she reached out to squeeze Robin's hand.

Robin returned the squeeze. "I'd send one of my kuckens home with you, but as you know, they sell out before noon every day."

"I'd rather eat one of your German kuckens than anything else I know of—even chocolate ice cream!" She whispered in her ear, "I am *so* fortunate to have you for my best friend!"

"Just wait until we start on the posters for vacation Bible school—you might change your mind! Don't forget, Friday at my house!"

"I won't forget," Dorine promised. "Oh, and Pastor Rick wants me to sing a solo in church Sunday, what do you suggest?" She and Robin had both taken piano lessons and sang together in high school, but Robin preferred playing to singing.

"I'll think of one and let you know—luckily, all I have to do is play a few chords here and there and you do all the rest!"

As she stepped out on the sidewalk, expecting to be blasted by the heat, Dorine was amazed at how the sky had changed while she had been inside— the dark clouds now billowed up to cover much of the sky overhead. Gusts of cool, rain-scented wind danced in the street, picking up pieces of paper and dust, swirling gracefully to unheard music. She took a deep breath, relishing the promise carried on the rain-washed air.

Hurrying to the pickup and sliding in, she caught the faint scent of Dean's cologne. Brushing her hand thoughtfully across the seat, she mulled over what Robin had said. Could her friend see something in Dean's personality that she didn't? She backed out on the wide street and turned to drive westward out of town.

The clouds rose up ahead of her like an angry genie out of his bottle, and the wind gusted against the pickup. Music always helped her think, and she reached over to twirl the radio dial. Dean liked western music and she didn't mind it, but right now she needed something for her soul. As she searched for the Christian station, she heard the deep rumble of thunder over the radio static.

Just as she turned off the pavement to the DeFoe ranch, the first fat raindrops fell. In another few minutes, the familiar *ping ping* of hailstones began hitting the top of the pickup. Turning on the windshield wipers, she peered through the gathering gloom with the same feeling of anxiety she'd had yesterday on the way home from college. Goodness! Was it only *yesterday?!!* It felt like ages ago!

By the time she drove into the yard, the hailstones were larger and falling faster. She parked under the trees, jumped out and gave the door a mighty shove to close it before sprinting towards the house. Lightning flickered overhead, followed by a booming crash that shook cold raindrops from the trembling cottonwood leaves.

"Shake a leg, there, cowgirl!" called Darrell from where he held the screendoor open. "Run!" In the gloom behind him, Marci and Mrs. Mac were crowded together, watching the storm.

"Ow! Ow!" Dorine yelped as she ran full speed up the sidewalk, the hailstones and heavy rain pelting her furiously.

"Hurry, dear, hurry!" anxiously called out Marci. Breathless and rain-drenched, Dorine dashed full bore into the entryway as Darrell stepped aside to let her in.

"You little dummy! You should have stayed in the pickup till this blew over!" he scolded in good-natured exasperation.

"Did you get bruised, dear?" Marci examined Dorine's bare arms.

"I don't think so, but man, am I wet!" Mrs. Mac had already grabbed a towel for Dorine's face and hair, making clucking sounds.

"Get out of those wet clothes before you catch cold!" ordered Darrell. He sounded so much like Dean that she turned to him and scowled. "Do you take lessons from your bossy brother?!!"

"Is he bossy? I hadn't noticed." Darrell's eyes twinkled, then he lifted one eyebrow and studied her. So low that the others couldn't hear, he asked, "Don't you get along with my bossy big brother? Is that what caused the ruckus today?" The questions came along with speculation in his deep blue eyes.

She blushed and glanced at the other women, who had turned

their attention back to the outdoors when another crack of lightning sounded nearby. Hailstones, larger now, hit the metal roofs on nearby buildings, roaring like a waterfall. Drenching rain poured straight down, gutters unable to hold the flood of water.

"I'm sorry you had to witness that this morning," she replied softly, stepping farther into the sunroom. "We both lost our tempers and before we knew it, we were yelling at each other. Oh, Darrell," she looked at him with pleading eyes, "how am I ever to witness of God's love to him if *I* can't show it?" She turned to go into the kitchen.

He sobered and shook his head as he walked slowly behind her. "I don't know, Dorine, I quit talking but I doubled my praying the day he told me to shut up, he didn't want to hear about God...Mother is the only one he respects enough to listen. He even plans it so he's not around when she and Mrs. Mac have their devotions. When she had that pneumonia, and no strength to hold the Bible, she asked him to read to her from the Psalms, and he did. His voice seemed to soothe her, but as soon as he saw she drifted off to sleep, he put the Bible down like it was a snake, couldn't wait to drop it."

Dorine finished drying her arms and wrapped the towel around her wet hair, turban-style. "He's *bothered* by what's in the Psalms, knowing it's the truth, and he doesn't want to hear it. He probably figures he doesn't have to deal with it if he doesn't hear it."

The phone rang and Darrell reached over to pick it up. "Yeah, she's here," his eyes flickered over Dorine, then he held the receiver away as a loud crackle came over the line. "Wow! That was close! We shouldn't be on the phone during this lightning, we'll get electrocuted!" After he hung up, he said unnecessarily, "That was Dean, wanting to know if you were all right. He called Robin as soon as it started to hail and she said you'd left but he was worried you might have slid off the road if it got slick from the hail...you know, he *does* worry about you a lot." He sent her a shrewd look.

"When pigs fly!" She retorted—then remembered her new vow and softened her voice. "Actually, you're the second one to tell me that today...but for now, I'm getting into some dry clothes!"

Darrell's gaze followed her as she left the room, and he speculated on the strong emotions he'd witnessed today between her and his big brother. *Hum-m-m, I wonder just what is going on here....this bears some watching...* and he smiled to himself.

Since the electricity had gone off, Mrs. Mac used the old wood stove to cook their supper that night. Dorine thought she secretly enjoyed it, as that was the way she'd cooked years ago. When Dean came in, she felt his eyes on her as she set the table, and raised her eyes to lock gazes with him before he turned away, removing his hat to hang it up. That look made her nervous and her palms grew sweaty—what should she say? Should she say *anything*?

If she had only known the control he was exerting—he wanted to go around the table and pick her up in his arms and kiss her breathless! She looked even more beautiful in the lamplight, her brown eyes reflecting deep pools of mystery, and red glints reflecting off her thick hair that he itched to run his hands through! Instead, he waited patiently while Darrell asked the blessing, passing dishes around the table afterwards. Dorine studiously avoided his glance but felt his presence as strongly as if he was touching her.

The storm had blown over by the time they'd finished eating and the brothers went to the barns to check for damage. Dorine helped with the dishes, then went to her room and began sorting through her bags. The lights suddenly flickered on, dispelling the shadows. But in her mind's eye, she could still see Dean, how the lamplight had cast shadows across his face, a face filled with character, kindness and tenderness. Her heart felt a tug and she wondered what would happen if she let her heart have its way...

Coming across her Bible, she lovingly fingered it—how many times had she used it to witness these past few years? Her dad had given it to her when she was ten, shortly after she'd accepted Jesus as her Savior. Opening the well-thumbed pages to her favorite book, the Psalms, she read, "I will proclaim Thy name to my brethren, in the midst of the congregation I will sing Thy praise. And again, I will put my trust in Him."

She looked up from the page. Dean was her "brethren," but she'd sure done a lousy job today of proclaiming His Name to him, she thought wryly. Sighing, she closed the book, laying it on the nightstand. *Lord, I keep coming to you in prayer about this, and most of the time, I'm getting victory over my tongue and temper, but I'm a long ways from conquering it...I give this burden to You once again.*

Laying in bed, staring up at the ceiling, she acknowledged that thoughts of Dean had taken over her mind—in fact, she realized with a start, that even the vandalism had receded; almost every waking thought was of Dean. How had he come to take up such a prominent place in her head? She sighed as her eyelids drooped, gradually slipping into a deep sleep.

The next morning, Dorine woke well after sunrise, and grumbling at her lateness, she dressed quickly, hoping to have breakfast with the family. She found only Marci and Mrs. Mac at the table, with coffee cups and open Bibles before them.

Marci smiled lovingly at her. "The boys were anxious to get started on breaking the new colts this morning, Dean said he'd be in the office later."

Dorine walked past them towards the coffee pot, putting her hand on Mrs. Mac's shoulder when the older woman started to rise. "I can get my own breakfast, Mrs. Mac, you don't have to wait on me."

The older woman crisply replied, "That's one of the joys in life, girl, doing for others." Her husband died before they'd had children, and she'd poured her life and love into the DeFoe children and any others that had need of her. A flush swept up her neck as Dorine brushed a kiss across her velvety cheek.

"So let me do for you once," Dorine whispered.

After breakfast and prayer around the table, she poured a cup of coffee, taking it with her as she left for the office.

Hearing the ranch hands cheering over at the corral, she veered from her path and went around the barn towards the corral to watch horse and man in an age-old battle of wills.

Dean stood by the head of a nervous sorrel gelding, talking soothingly. Two of the ranch hands held the animal's tossing head.

The other men were perched on corral posts or draped their arms over the railing, waiting to watch the fun when Dean climbed on the unbroken horse.

Slowly, he slid his hands over the sleek neck and moved to the side, the horse snorting and throwing its head as he tried to turn and watch the man. Taking the reins, Dean reached up for the saddle horn and quickly swung into the saddle. "Let 'em go!" he yelled, and the two hands jumped back out of the way.

The horse exploded, ducking its head and springing up in the air, kicking its heels in an effort to dislodge the hated burden from its back. "Ee-haw-w, ride 'em, boss!" yelled Buster. The horse jumped and fish-tailed its body, bucking all over the corral. Dean stuck to the saddle like a burr, one arm in the air, his hat going flying to land in the trampled dust. The men hooted and shouted encouragement as the horse furiously tried to buck Dean off. The animal came closer and closer to the railings and just when Dorine thought it would crush Dean against the corral poles, he grabbed a post, pulling himself out of the saddle. The horse continued to buck, moving away as Dean dropped to the ground. He strode over to pick up his hat and dust it off while Darrell roped the horse and snugged the lariat around a post before the animal could rear. Dorine realized she'd been holding her breath—she'd seen Dean break horses before, but his form today had been *awesome*! She watched muscles bunch across his broad shoulders and back when he leaned over to pick up his hat, his shirt sweat-stained as he grimly moved towards the horse. Buster had another rope on the quivering animal as it rolled its eyes wildly, watching for the hated man. Dean approached, talking calmly and stroking the horse's sweaty neck. The horse threw its head in the air and tried to rear, but Darrell hauled on the rope and yanked the animal back to the ground.

Dean took that opportunity to grab the reins and climb in the saddle. The men let go and the horse backed up, then lunged and dipped it's head between it's front legs, kicking out with its back feet, sending Dean sailing over it's head, landing on the ground on his side with a whump! Dorine winced and clutched the cup, but relaxed when Dean got up, a determined look on his face as he crammed his hat tighter on his head.

Darrell laughed and ran forward to catch the reins, watching for the churning hooves of the still-bucking horse. "What's the matter, Dean! Did you push the eject button?!!" The men hooted and hollered, applauding when Dean climbed back on the animal. Again, it lunged and dipped its head, but this time, Dean was ready and kept his seat, even though his hat went sailing again. The sun caught in his wildly blowing hair, glinting off the black strands. His body was athletic and supple, settling into the rhythm of the bucking animal. What a magnificent display of strength, Dorine thought, by both man and animal. Why hadn't she ever paid attention to how thoroughly masculine and strong Dean was?...how *sexy*—she yanked her thoughts to a stop—what was the *matter* with her! Turning abruptly, she hurried to the office, furiously concentrating on what she had to do there, to keep her growing feelings from taking over her mind altogether!

Dean came in and out of the office several times that day, but she studiously kept her eyes on the computer screen. However, she didn't *need* to look—every fiber in her being stood at attention when he was in the room! She tried to subdue her quickened heartbeat, but it wouldn't quiet. Taking several shallow breaths, she finally gave in to the tidal wave of emotion...was she actually *attracted* to him?!! She couldn't! He was just being nice and "neighborly" as he put it—she shouldn't try to read anymore into it than that. She shook her head as though to clear any romantic notions out—it was all *Robin's* fault she was entertaining these thoughts!

Dean had a lot of crow to eat about his reaction to Dorine's guest ranch idea, but he wasn't used to apologizing. Number one, he was the boss—he was pretty much in control of situations and seldom had to back down. He admired that she was a strong, independent woman, no longer that coltish, unsure teenager he'd seen off to college over four years ago. She had blossomed into a self-confident woman who knew what she wanted out of the future. But why had she shut him out of it? He'd *always* been there for her! Her accusation that he was trying to control her tore at his heart—was that the way she saw it?

Sitting at his office desk, he absently rubbed his sore ribs—he'd never got bucked off the other day if it hadn't been for that one second when he'd seen her and lost concentration. Now he stared unseeingly at an aerial photograph of the ranch on the far wall—he'd never considered Dorine as an independent adult, he was still seeing her as that fearful-eyed young girl on the day of her father's funeral, the day he silently vowed he would protect her and always be there for her—but *had* he overstepped the line between protection and control?

He didn't like the image he was getting of himself. Mentally kicking himself, he turned his chair and looked out the window at the prairie beyond, where soft breezes bent the wild grasses. And just like the breeze, was he trying to bend Dorine to *his* will? He had to admit that Dorine had done her homework when it came to the details of operating a guest ranch—but why didn't she *say* anything? He'd always felt so important in her life—he knew *everything* about her—even her social security number! She indicated she had been researching the subject for two years—*two years!* And never once hinted what she was considering. It hurt that she had made the decision without consulting him. It wasn't even annoyance, he finally had to admit, it was hurt.

But, why should it? It didn't have anything to do with him—she had no way of knowing of his feelings, how even a hint of a smile from her stirred his heart. He loved everything about her—her warm personality, her graciousness, her mannerisms, her laughter—but she seldom laughed around him anymore. He mulled that over—he needed to bring back that laughter, needed her to relax around him again. As he started on the waiting paperwork, he realized he had his work cut out for him!

# CHAPTER EIGHT

The phone ringing at his elbow interrupted his train of thought and he listened to the plaintive voice on the other end. "All right, I'll be right over." He hung up and reached for his hat.

Heading out the door, he glanced at Hazel. "That was Crawford, he thinks some of our cattle got through the fence so I'm going over there." Hazel nodded in understanding. Usually he sent one of the men, but with this rustling business, he wanted to see for himself. He slid his gaze towards Dorine, but she appeared to be in deep concentration at the computer. That saucy curl at the end of her long braid beckoned, and he rammed his hat on, turning his thoughts off.

Getting into his pickup, he backed it up while he wrenched his thoughts to more practical matters— the fact that the rustlers may have surfaced again—had they cut the fences but got scared off before they could take the cattle? Or had the cattle just found a weak spot and pushed through?

He'd driven for only a short distance when he realized his favorite station wasn't on the radio—Dorine must have changed it when she drove the pickup yesterday. As he reached for the dial, the announcer's voice stayed his hand. "Have you ever hated God? Stay tuned for the following program and interesting insights into this question!" Dean's hand dropped to his thigh.

The announcer's question brought him up short. *Did he hate God?* How *did* he think of that Mighty Being? Hatred?…no…he didn't actually *hate* God—it was just that God didn't care anymore, so why should he bother caring about Him?!! Irritated that the Christian announcer had caused his thoughts to go that direction, he put the radio back on the western music station, shoving away thoughts of God.

The pickup bumped along the fence line through the pasture to where he found a weak post that had fallen over, allowing the cattle to tromp through. However, his mind wasn't on what he was doing— the radio preacher's words nagged at him, made him angry—why was God *always* butting into his business?

Taking a metal post, sledgehammer and wire stretcher from the back of the pickup, he set about making temporary repairs. But the announcer's voice kept hounding him—*did he hate God?* Sandwiched between God and Dorine—he was beginning to feel like a slice of salami! He knew she was a dedicated Christian and her life showed it. He pounded the post into the ground—but how could she continue to worship an uncaring God? Stretching the wire, he thought about his mother, Mrs. Mac and even Darrell, faithfully worshipping and praying—he shook his head. Was *he* the only one out of step?

The sharp jab of a barb on the wire brought him up short. Taking his glove off, he put his finger in his mouth where the blood was oozing—See! If he hadn't been thinking about this non-caring God, he wouldn't have jabbed himself! Drawing his glove back on, he put God on the back burner where He'd been kept for years, and turned his attention to finishing the repair job.

Driving back across the pasture and through Crawford's yard, he rolled to a stop by the barn where his lanky neighbor worked on a disassembled hay rake. "I'll be sending some of the guys over to get the cattle later," he called out the window. "Thanks for keeping them in your corral."

Crawford glanced up and absently waved a greasy hand. "Glad to oblige."

Dean drove home, turning the radio up louder and singing along to the wailing western song to drown out his thoughts about God.

The next morning, he flew to meet a client in Nebraska. He paid strict attention to what he was doing at takeoff and landing to keep from making any mistakes, but when he was airborne, thoughts of the vibrant brunette immediately took up residence again. She'd flown with him countless times, he could almost imagine her sitting here with him. She was independent, strong in her convictions and so beautiful, both inside and out. He didn't want to antagonize her anymore, but how could he keep her from danger if she were to move back over to her place? He didn't want her over there by herself—

what if the vandals came back and decided to finish the job by destroying the house? And with her in it? He shuddered at the thought and found he was gripping the controls so tightly his knuckles were white.

His well-ordered life was now as full of ups and downs as the sky he flew through, and for once, he felt himself floundering—it was like hitting an air pocket and losing control. He smiled grimly—what would *that* look like, for the president of Flying Farmers to crack up his own plane, just because he couldn't keep his mind off a woman!

Dorine poked her head in the TV room to tell the two older women that she was going to Robin's to make posters for Bible school. "Have a good time! Be sure to roll up your windows, it looks like rain!" called Marci, without taking her eyes off the screen.

Steve had repaired her car but warned that she needed to trade it in soon for a newer model. Yeah, right—what would she use for money? Always praying for safety before she drove anywhere, this time was no different—she breathed a prayer of thanks when the car actually started!

It was relaxing to be with Robin and her boys, Jason and Jeremy, who shyly accepted Dorine's presence. As the evening wore on, they gradually warmed up to her, and by their bedtime, they insisted that Dorine give them their baths, to which she agreed. "Do you know what you're getting into?" Robin asked, her eyes dancing with mischief.

"What's so hard about giving baths to a two-year-old and a three-year-old?" Dorine scoffed.

"Don't say I didn't warn you!" gaily laughed Robin.

An hour later, the boys were bathed and dressed in pajamas—but Dorine was damp from head to toe. She laughed along with Robin about her initiation into bath time, then sat at the end of the bed as Robin read to the boys and prayed with them. Robin kissed them goodnight, but Jeremy glanced shyly at Dorine. "Can Auntie Reen kiss me too?" he pleaded.

Something melted in Dorine's heart and she quickly went to the sweet little boy. Jason also gave her an expectant glance.

"I've got kisses and hugs for you too," she whispered. It wasn't long until they drifted off to sleep, and the women tip-toed out of the room and down the hall to the front room.

"You are so blest, Robin," Dorine said sincerely.

"I know," Robin agreed, a Madonna-like expression on her face. "It's funny, when I think back to high school, how important all those teen things were, like the prom, football games and whether we had dates for Saturday night…but it all fades in comparison to what I have now." Her eyes traveled over Dorine's face. "Those same blessings are waiting for you too, Dorine."

With a wistful expression, Dorine replied, "I've never wanted to do anything but live on the ranch, have a loving husband, a happy marriage and children…but, nothing is happening!"

"Well, girl, you need to get off your duff and doing something about it!" her friend observed bluntly.

As Dorine picked up a marker to start on the posters, she replied, "I always thought I'd meet the man of my dreams in college, or through rodeo contacts, but…" she shrugged, "I've never met anyone yet who I'd like to spend the rest of my life with."

"How about—"

"Don't even go there!" Dorine snorted. "*That* would be like marrying my brother!"

"Dean doesn't look at you like a brother, believe me!"

"You need glasses—all *he* wants is control."

"I wonder…" Robin laughed softly.

"If you don't quit, I'll go home and you can do these yourself!"

Robin chuckled and prudently dropped the subject. After they finished the posters, they practiced several songs before Dorine left.

As she drove the empty road toward the ranch, Dorine leaned her elbow on the open window and with her fingers, thoughtfully twisted a piece of her long hair. Being with Robin was soothing, and singing praises to the Lord always uplifted her more than anything she had ever experienced.

Deep in thought as she drove into the DeFoe yard, she turned off the motor and gazed at the big, century-old house. A sturdily-built log and native stone structure, it had been tastefully added on to several times, and had withstood a number of tornadoes—it looked as though it could stand another hundred years. The huge cottonwoods surrounding it stretched out protective leafy branches, providing a safe haven for all...including her...for now.

Dorine was helping Marci and Mrs. Mac get ready for the party Saturday, in spite of their objections that she shouldn't, since she was the guest of honor.

The two brothers set up the barbecue and got steaks ready to grill. Both dressed in long shorts covering their swim suits, and Dorine couldn't take her eyes off Dean's broad chest and muscular arms. Wrestling cattle and handling heavy hay bales had resulted in a well-toned body, but to cover her interest, she resorted to humor as she teased them about scorching the hair on their chests when they started to cook.

Dean smiled mysteriously with no comment, but Darrell slapped his chest. "Hey, it took me a long time to grow this, you think I want to jeopardize it?" She laughed and escaped back into the house, aware of Dean's eyes on her.

Guests arrived, and Dorine took her place beside Marci to welcome them. Mrs. Mac kept everyone supplied with appetizers as she invited them back to the poolside tables. When Melody and Paul arrived with baby Kimberly, Dorine took the tiny infant, the baby powder scent creating a yearning in Dorine's heart. Contented baby snores touched an instinct deep within her and she wondered if she would ever experience this joy?

She was unaware of Dean watching how natural she looked with the baby, a naked wistfulness on her face. She would make an excellent mother, he had no doubt, and at the thought that he would like to be the father of those babies, a desire to hold her curled through him. But he needed to bide his time—she still didn't have a clue as to his feelings, and he had to take it slow.

Dorine reluctantly handed the baby back to her mother, turning to greet Robin and her children, followed by the pastor and his family.

Neighbors and friends arrived in a steady stream. There was a blur of people and she felt overwhelmed at the warmth and generosity of her townspeople. Did Marci say "just a few" friends and neighbors?—the whole countryside was here!

After everyone had stuffed themselves, Dorine was guided to the gift-laden table amid good-natured joking and conversation. Dean stood next to Marietta Kingston, the postmaster, both of them holding tall glasses of iced tea. He couldn't keep his eyes off Dorine—she was stunning in a modest turquoise bathing suit with a matching, long, wraparound skirt. She'd worn her hair down, the shimmering strands held in place with a turquoise silk flower, from which the soft mahogany curls drifted invitingly across her bare shoulders. Dean had to keep reminding himself that he could only give her "brotherly" touches. He'd learned to master his expression in years of heading up the family business, but when it came to Dorine, he wasn't sure the tight control would stay in place.

Among the gifts was a memory album from Robin, a fashionable western skirt with fringe from Marci and Mrs. Mac, a recent popular Christian book from Darrell, but her hands shook when she came to the tiny package from Dean. Carefully unwrapping it, she stared at the silver charm bracelet, with tiny horses, saddles and other western figures. She examined each one until she came to the end—there was a tiny heart with the letter "D" engraved on it. She raised her eyes shyly to meet Dean's gaze and smiled appreciatively. He nodded and winked, sending a blush over her cheeks. It was getting harder and harder for her to resist the attraction she felt at the tender looks from those incredible eyes! She didn't remember ever feeling so off-balance around *anyone*!

After the wrappings were put away, a lively game of water ball was followed by races. Darrell challenged any and all, having been on his college championship swim team. Dorine swam on one team, which came in second, and as she turned to boost herself up, strong hands reached for hers. She looked up to see Dean waiting with an inviting smile.

Hesitantly, she placed her hands in his. With seemingly no effort, he lifted her straight up out of the water to stand in front of him. "You don't weigh very much, even dripping wet." His hands at her waist sent shivers down her legs...or could it be just the cool air?

At that moment, several exuberant teens bumped against them, catching Dean off-balance. With flailing arms, over he went into the pool. Dorine barely kept her own balance, laughing delightedly at the look of chagrin on his face as he surfaced. He grinned at her and shook the water out of his hair, blinking as he tread water. He looked so endearing, she wanted to jump into the pool and throw her arms around his neck—

She gasped and put her hand over her mouth—*what was wrong with her?—he'd think she'd lost her mind!*

As twilight dropped its soft mantel, the pool lights came on, creating a romantic background to couples still in the water. Soon, however, older people drifted inside and younger couples with sleepy children said their farewells and left.

Dorine eventually found herself alone with Dean, stacking plates and clearing the table. Neither had changed out of their swimsuits, although Dorine had put her wraparound skirt on. She wished Dean had put a shirt on, too—she was achingly aware of his bare chest even though he had a towel draped around his neck. As he paused beside her, every fiber of her body noticed, her hands trembling so much she knocked over a stack of cups. "Here comes Grace!" she joked, in an attempt to hide her nervousness.

"Leave it," he said softly, his touch light on her arm. She turned and looked up into those beautiful brilliant blue eyes. He seemed to be waiting...waiting for? Then comprehension dawned.

"I didn't get the chance to thank you properly for my gift," she indicated the bracelet jangling on her arm. "It was very thoughtful of you." She sounded as breathless as she felt, her heart fluttering wildly—*get a grip, Dorine!!*

"There's no one around now, you can thank me *properly*."

She searched his eyes, not daring to think of what he was asking...did he want her to *kiss* him?!! He remained very still, his hands on her waist...*when had he moved them there?* Taking a deep breath, she reached up quickly and pecked him on the cheek.

"There! Thank you, Mr. DeFoe." Her light-hearted remark faded away in the face of the tender, teasing look he gave her.

"That wasn't good enough, prairie chick," he murmured softly, sliding his arms around her. *Forget this brotherly stuff.* He lowered his face towards her.

"Wh-what do you mean?" she stuttered nervously, laying her hands on his bare chest at a feeble attempt to widen the distance between them. Jolts of awareness zinged up her arms and she looked at him helplessly. This was totally foreign territory to her and she had *no* idea what she was supposed to do.

"You *could* thank me like this," and he lightly brushed her lips with his. Lightning jolts flashed along her nerves and she took shallow breaths. He drew back to give her a chance to retreat but she stood as still as a deer caught in the headlights of his pickup. Her brown eyes were wide, filled with questions and an expectation that drove out all his restraints.

He touched her lips again and when she remained motionless, he brought her closer and deepened the kiss. His bare hands on her back gently caressed her in a slow circular movement. Every dream he'd had of kissing her paled in the reality of her soft, desirable lips against his—his thundering heart seconded the motion!

Dorine could scarcely breathe, and without further thought, her arms slid up across his broad shoulders and around his neck, returning the kiss. Any coherent thoughts she had rocketed off into space, as her world narrowed to his warm lips on hers. She had seldom kissed her dates, so had no frame of reference for the earth-shattering emotions reeling through her. The party faded into oblivion—there were no people in the house, there were no plates to clear, only the feel of Dean's strong arms around her, cherishing her in an exquisite fantasy of just the two of them.

Then a small inner voice intruded—*what are you doing?!!* Reality returned like cold water dumped on her and she jerked back, her hands resting on his forearms. Surprised that her feet were still solidly on the ground, she drew in a deep breath. Gazing up into his desire-darkened eyes, she whispered, "Why did you do that?"

"You say thank you in a *very* proper way," he murmured in a ragged voice, leaning his forehead on hers. She was such an innocent! She had no idea of how delectable she was.

"You've never kissed me....like...that," her voice trembled as she tried to draw away. He held her firmly, his cheek brushing her temple. More now than ever, he cherished her innocence.

"You've never graduated from college before either," he hesitated, then continued, "*Have* you been kissed a lot?" His voice came more gruffly than he intended, and he was amazed at the wave of jealousy that swept over him.

"No," she replied breathlessly. "At least, not like...you...." Her hands fluttered nervously and she looked everywhere but at him.

"You don't have to be nervous around me, prairie chick." His voice softened, filled with a gentle tenderness she'd never heard.

She took several shallow breaths but before she could formulate a cohesive sentence, Darrell's voice intruded. "Hey, you two gonna take all night to clear that table?!!"

Dorine jerked out of Dean's embrace, and with a mortified glance in his direction, she grabbed the nearest stack of plates to carry into the house, brushing past Darrell on his way out.

Dean stood looking after her, his heart throbbing furiously, then he turned, whipped the towel off from around his neck and took a running dive into the pool. Swimming underwater to the other end to cool off, his thoughts churned like the water around him. He had never expected such an earth-shaking explosion when he touched her lips, but he'd felt that kiss clear through his very being! He had wanted to kiss her lovable lips ever since she was 16—*never* in his wildest dreams had he expected it to be so electrifying!

He surfaced and wiped the water out of his eyes, throwing his head back to get the hair off his forehead. "Hooee," he breathed.

"Hey," Darrell's plaintive voice floated over the pool to him. "I could sure use some help folding up these tables!"

"Yeah, in a minute." He watched Darrell take tablecloths off, but there was *no way* he was going anywhere near him at the moment. His deeply imbedded moral values had just taken a severe bashing and it shook him to his core. He'd always prided himself on how well he handled his life, yes, took *pride* in his self-control, but in one instant, Dorine had shaken that self-control to its foundation—and she had no idea of her power over him!

He knew himself well enough to know that now he could not trust himself around her. She was so innocent, the guileless way she'd returned his kiss—now, more than ever, he had to protect her...from himself.

# CHAPTER NINE

Dorine hoped that she appeared normal to everyone in the kitchen, but later, she couldn't remember clearing up the dishes, and bidding guests farewell was a foggy memory. She quickly excused herself to Marci, saying she was tired after such a full day. Marci's eyes followed her up the stairs, the older woman thoughtful.

Laying in bed, Dorine gingerly touched her lips and felt Dean's kiss again. Her heart quickened at the tenderness with which he'd held her but she was completely unnerved by his actions. Total confusion reigned—what had happened to her solid convictions of his "black" character?!! She'd often been in his arms at 4-H square dance demonstrations, but then he'd always been teasing and "brotherly"— was she reading too much into that kiss? People's emotions were usually uninhibited when they were relaxed—could *that* be what prompted Dean to kiss her? Because her own emotions had been on a roller coaster ride this past week, could *that* be why she had responded to him? So many questions, all clamoring to be answered at once—it made her mind whirl! When she was a child, it had seemed natural for him to kiss and cuddle her when she fell and skinned her knee—but the kiss they'd shared tonight was nothing like a "make-it-well kiss"—it went *'way* beyond comparison!

Turning on her side, she punched her pillow, remembering the girlish talks she and her classmates had had in their dorm rooms.

Some of her friends were engaged to be married, and with stars in their eyes, had told about the love and security they'd felt when held tightly in the embrace of their beloved. Dorine had never been able to contribute to those conversations because she'd never felt that kind of attraction for anyone. A woman had to feel something in common with a man...didn't she? *You and Dean have lots in common*, whispered a little voice—love of family, ranching, rodeo—her thoughts abruptly ended—there was *one* area, the most important one, that they *didn't* share—love of the Lord. If, and it was a big "if," he really felt something for her, what could come of it?

She switched on the lamp and reached for her Bible. "Come to Me and I will give you rest; cast your cares upon Me, My yoke is easy, My burden is light."

Closing her eyes, she prayed that God would help her sort out her thoughts and make clear her paths. Closing the Bible, she switched off the light and lay staring up at the ceiling. If only Dean hadn't teased her so much about waiting for her to grow up so he could marry her. She tossed restlessly, turning over and wished she knew more about men. But she acknowledged that God had protected her and guided her in pure paths so that she could bring an innocent bride to her husband on their wedding night. It was a long time before she fell asleep...and her dreams were filled with a certain tall rancher with the bluest of blue eyes.

Sunday morning, Dorine woke slowly, reluctant to leave her dream—a dark-haired hero was brushing his lips tantalizingly over hers. Her eyes drifted opened, bringing the sharp focus of reality—had Dean *really* kissed her so passionately last night? It was *so* out of character for him...wasn't it? He *surely* wouldn't tease her like that....*would he*?!! And even worse, how would he act towards her this morning? How should *she* act? Totally confused, she wondered how, overnight, he'd turned from her antagonist, into...what? *What* exactly *was* he now?!! Fingering the bracelet he'd given her last night, she delicately touched each little figure, wondering why she was wearing it, considering who gave it to her.

While she showered and dressed, she wondered if she could face him this morning. Should she act like his teasing didn't bother her? And that *kiss*! If he *was* only teasing, what would a *real* kiss be like?!! She closed her eyes, tasting again the warmth of his lips, reliving the feeling of having his arms around her, holding her, cherishing her—her eyes snapped open! *What foolishness!*

Wearing a simply-styled cotton lavender dress, with white strappy high heels and a daisy-chain necklace, she ran a brush through her hair, letting it curl softly as it cascaded down her back. Gazing in the mirror, she tilted her chin up—she would stay cool and collected, treat Dean the same as always. Giving herself a reassuring nod, she picked up her Bible and purse.

Going down to breakfast, her good intentions went right out the window when she saw Dean in a dark, well-fitted navy western suit that turned his eyes even more blue. *When* had he become so appealing and handsome?!! She paused in the doorway, her eyes devouring him.

He glanced at her as he sat down. "Good morning." Even though his tone was friendly, his face was expressionless. At least he was giving her a cue; she would respond with equal politeness.

"Good morning." Walking quickly to the coffee pot, she reached for a cup, hearing him snap open the <u>Rapid City Journal</u>. *He was ignoring her*! She took a deep breath as disappointment washed over her—he acted as though she was a stick of furniture! Her heart dropped into her stomach and her hands trembled so she could hardly hold her cup as she poured the hot liquid.

Marci came into the room, fastening her earrings. "Good morning, dears!" Dean whistled at his mother and a faint blush stole over her cheeks. She stopped abruptly as she noticed his suit and tie.

He sipped his coffee and gave her an innocent look. "Dorine's singing in church today, it's been a long time since I heard her."

Dorine flushed with pleasure but sneaking a peak at him, all she could see was the back of the newspaper. Darrell clattered down the stairs but stopped short when he saw Dean dressed for church. It was just a slight hesitation, but his eyes sought out Dorine's and she saw the question repeated there that was in her own heart.

After breakfast, they filed out to the large ranch van and much to Dorine's consternation, Marci followed Mrs. Mac into the back and Darrell got in, pulling the side door shut. Turning questioning eyes to Dean, she saw he was patiently holding open the front passenger door, waiting for her. "Your mother—?"

"Is already in the back," he finished as he took her elbow and helped her up. His fingers left a tingling when he stepped back and shut the door. She glanced nervously over her shoulder to meet Darrell's gaze twinkling with humor. She quickly turned around and stared ahead as they drove down the lane. Conversation swirled around her as the others talked about looking forward to friends and neighbors they hadn't seen all week. It felt as though her tongue was stuck to the roof of her mouth and for the life of her, she couldn't think of a single thing to say. Dean too, was more quiet than usual, but when she chanced a glance at him, his eyes were on the road ahead and she could tell nothing from his expression.

After greeting other worshipers near the church steps, the ringing of the steeple bell summoned them to enter and file into the pews.

When it was time for her solo, Dorine walked to the piano where Robin was already playing the introduction to her song. As Dorine poured out her worship to the Lord in a clear soprano voice, she closed her eyes and lifted her heart to the heavens. She sang of God's love and His all-caring watch over His lambs. For those moments, she forgot all about Dean, forgot about her vandalized house, forgot everything except the love for Jesus that welled up.

Dean listened to her lovely sweet voice, drawn reluctantly into worship by her adoration of the Father. For a moment, that niggling doubt returned to his mind—*had* he been wrongly accusing God? The inviting words of the song plucked at his soul, wound themselves around his heart and entered every fiber of his being. Dorine looked beautifully ethereal, as though she had been transported into a realm where he could never go, and a deep loneliness swept over him.

Then the song ended, and he came back to earth, was once again sitting in this little country church, being caught up by emotion towards a God he didn't trust. His little trip a moment ago was just the result of a skillful song-writer, he told himself.

Following the last note, there was a hushed awe over the congregation, then Pastor Rick began applauding, a wide smile on his beaming face. Others joined in and Dorine dipped her head in acknowledgment. She didn't want their applause, and would never get used to people clapping after such a reverent number, but was gracious enough to accept it in the spirit in which it was given. Chancing a glance at Dean as she walked down the aisle to her seat, she noticed his tight smile, the skeptical glitter back in his eyes as he applauded with everyone else. Her heart sank. *Lord, let his heart ponder the music, and open his thoughts to the message today.*

She slipped into the pew beside Mrs. Mac and Marci, thankful that Dean was on the other side of them. He had turned his attention to the pastor's message. Dorine was very conscious of his every move, when he crossed his booted feet, when he put his arm on the pew back behind his mother. She could just see his hand if she looked to the side. It was a strong hand, capable, his fingernails clean and cut bluntly. He occasionally drummed his fingertips on the back of the pew and she wondered if he was even listening to Pastor Rick. Her Bible was open on her lap, but she had difficulty concentrating. *Oh, Lord, You are my God…please let him know You are his God too.*

The message was direct and simple, offering a haven of rest to all who would come to Him. Pastor Rick, a middle-aged man with a deep commitment to the Lord, led his congregation through a series of points to emphasize the Father's love toward mankind. Dean's fingers stilled a couple of times when pastor mentioned God's love was expressed by His Son dying on the cross.

If only Dean would open himself up again! During prayer time, she fervently asked that his cold heart be warmed by the knowledge that God loved him, God loved Dean DeFoe…and cared about him more than anyone on this earth ever could.

After church, they returned to the ranch for dinner, but Dean took extra care not to touch her as she walked ahead of him into the house. She stole a sideways glance at him, but his face was shuttered and he merely smiled at her.

He saw the hurt look in her eyes and almost reached out to her, but knew that if he did, he'd be tempted to tell her that he couldn't live without her, that he wanted her by his side forever. That sort of declaration would probably send her packing. He'd have to dig deep for every ounce of self-control to maintain a "brotherly" attitude.

When they were through eating, Darrell stretched his arms over his head and yawned as he got up. "I'm gonna watch the ball game, anybody else want to?" He ambled off towards the television room.

"You'll be asleep before the first inning's over," scoffed Dean, putting his knife and fork across the edge of his plate.

Marci and Mrs. Mac both agreed that a nap did sound good, and no wonder, Dorine thought, all the work they did yesterday. While she helped them clear away the dishes, Dean stayed at the table with another cup of coffee, looking thoughtful.

"I'm riding Blaze over to check on my east fence line," Dorine said as she wiped her hands on a dishtowel. "On *this* side of the fence," she added pointedly.

Dean's gaze snapped to her face as a frown wedged between his dark brows. He wondered if she'd grasped how serious this situation was with the rustlers. "I'll go with you," he offered, then clamped his lips shut—*why did he say that?*

"No!" she answered quickly, "I don't want to interfere with your, er, plans, I'll be fine."

"Take the cell phone with you," he commanded as he stood.

Her temper began to rise but in deference to Marci, she said calmly, "I've been riding there for years, and never had a phone."

"This is different now." Dean's eyes held a frosty challenge.

She wondered if all men blew hot and cold—how was she supposed to keep up with his changing moods? But one kiss was not going to sway her—she would *not* allow him to tell her what to do!

"Yes, dear, he's right," chimed in Marci. "There never used to be much rural crime…but this is a different world we live in now."

Dorine dropped her gaze, not wanting to see the triumph in his, and swallowed her anger. She would never do anything to hurt Marci's feelings. "All right," she conceded shortly, turning towards the stairs.

Changing into jeans, a cool, long-sleeved cotton shirt and boots, she gathered a snack, water, sunglasses and her hat, then picked up the cell phone at the office. Dean's car was nowhere in sight—he was no doubt visiting his redhead! Her initial spurt of anger soon drained away and left her feeling hurt and disappointed. She *wished* he had never kissed her. No, she didn't—oh, she didn't know *what* to think now! That kiss had changed everything between them!

It was probably just as well she didn't know that Dean was

meeting with area law enforcement officers at Kadoka, who had evidence that was beginning to connect the vandalism with rustlers.

When she whistled for Blaze, he whinnied and came trotting, tossing his head and prancing. Momentarily forgetting her hurt, she laughed and talked lovingly to the horse as she saddled him. Walking him to the first gate, she opened it, led him through and shut it. Putting a foot in the stirrup, she swung up onto the horse's back, the leather saddle creaking as she settled herself and adjusted her hat.

Trotting the horse along the boundary fence between the two ranches, she realized she couldn't see part of her fence lines unless she went over there...with only a small twinge of guilt, she rode to the connecting gate—no one could see, no one would ever know.

It felt wonderful to gallop across the prairie, *her* prairie land, the wind in her face and the feel of the smooth-gaited horse beneath her—she put all thoughts out of her head except the enjoyment of the moment.

Blaze dropped into a trot after a time, breathing hard and she kept him moving to cool off until he was walking sedately along. The scorching sun beat down on her and heat waves radiated up from the ground in the distance. A bird sang in the bushes along the trail, and the rhythmic sound of the horse's hooves lulled her sleepily.

Farther and farther into the Badlands she rode, never ceasing to marvel at God's handiwork in the beautiful colors and formations. Why couldn't Dean see God's hand in creation? Maybe he did, but he completely avoided the subject, so how was one to know where he stood? Her thoughts came full circle, back to that wondrous, eye-opening kiss last night—*this had to stop*! Why couldn't she get him out of her mind?!!

Blaze followed a trail through dusty outcroppings, his ears pricked forward, eyes attentive to the trail, and she let the peacefulness of the scenery seep into her bones...lulling her...

Suddenly, a man wearing dark glasses stepped out in front of them, and Blaze reared in fright. Dorine clutched her legs against the horse's sides to keep her seat as her heart pounded frantically.

"Whoa! Whoa! Good boy, steady!" she soothed the frightened animal as he pranced around, head held high while his eyes rolled till their whites showed. "Whoa, boy, down, boy," she murmured as he shivered and flinched, turning to face the intruder.

The man, dressed in obviously new jeans, western shirt, shiny boots and clean felt hat, remained where he stood, watching with a sober expression. He was of average height and build, but his stance seemed menacing.

"Who are *you*?" she demanded as she finally managed to get Blaze under control. "What are you doing here?!!" The undertone of fear in her voice prompted Blaze to begin dancing sideways again, tossing his head and eyeing the stranger with wild looks. She tightened her grip on the reins as she talked softly to the gelding, making crooning, calming sounds, leaning forward to pat his neck.

Still, the man never moved. As she took another look at him, a trickle of fear skittered down her spine—could *this* be one of the rustlers? Could she get her pistol out before he realized what she was doing? Then what? Could she *really* shoot another human being? No, better to run—could she ride away before he reached her?

"The question, is, who are *you*?" he demanded in a curt voice.

"*You're* the one trespassing, this is *my* land!" She held tight to the reins while her other hand searched for the strap on the backpack.

He sent her a startled look. "*You're* Dorine Andrews?"

"Never mind—who are *you*?" she stated authoritatively while her trembling fingers undid the strap.

The man eased his rigid stance and tucked his thumbs in the belt loops of his jeans, a friendly expression replacing his steely hardness. "I'm Bryce Martin, the insurance investigator."

"You're—where's your proof?"

He slowly reached in his back pocket and brought out a wallet, snapping it open to show impressive-looking identification.

"What are you doing way out here?" Her shaking fingers stilled on the strap as her heart began to settle down.

He slid the wallet back into his pocket and removed his sunglasses. "So you *are* Dorine Andrews?" He appeared relaxed when she nodded but she knew he wasn't—his eyes didn't miss a thing, from the top of her head to her feet before sliding away to the countryside around them. Alert. That was the word.

She slowly forced herself to relax as she studied him— her hand was still on the backpack. "I didn't expect to see anyone out here."

He moved closer, eyeing the horse. "Will he bite?"

He looked so comical that humor began to replace her apprehension, and she took her hand from the backpack. Her reply, however, came out terse. "If you put your fingers between his teeth, he will!" She swung her leg over and stepped down to the ground.

Bryce's expression was sheepish as he approached, still keeping well away from the horse. He was the same height as she was, and as he came nearer, she noticed he had light brown eyes that were trained apprehensively on the horse. Robin's words about him being a "hunk" came to mind.

Dorine looked around. "How did you get out here? You sure didn't ride, did you?" Her gaze came back to rest on him skeptically.

He adopted an affronted stance. "What's the matter, don't you think I can ride?" She gave him a speaking glance, and he relented.

"No, I've got a Jeep parked over that last ridge. I've been out here off and on the last month."

"Looking for rustlers?" She almost had to laugh at how her blunt question caught him off guard, as she continued to stroke the horse's neck, calming him.

He chuckled. "Looking for *anything* that doesn't belong— tire tracks, a scrap of paper, cigarette stub, remains of a campfire." He took off his hat and swiped his shirtsleeve across his forehead. Dorine noticed how his light brown hair, stylishly cut, laid in damp waves. "Whew, it's hot out here! How do you stand it?!" He replaced the hat and gave her an admiring glance. "You don't look as hot as I feel!"

"I'm used to it—do you have any idea how badly you scared me?" she demanded suddenly.

"The element of surprise works both ways, doesn't it?" he shot right back at her.

"If my horse had thrown me, what would you have done then?"

Giving her a steely look, he replied, "But he didn't, you handled him admirably, so that's a moot question. Besides," he looked around, "I'm getting thirsty. I was just on the way back to my Jeep and some lunch." At her tightlipped look, he looked abashed and offered her a tentative smile. "All right, I'm sorry! I didn't know who you were, okay?" He watched indecision flit over her face, then her expression cleared—he was off the hook.

"So, have you had lunch? Want to share mine?" He slipped his sunglasses back on.

"I've already eaten, thanks, but I'll walk with you." She followed him towards the nearby ridge, leading Blaze. "Have you found anything suspicious yet?"

He wondered how much he should tell her. "A couple of weeks ago, there were some truck tire tracks back over there," he waved vaguely off towards their right, "but after following them for quite a ways, I didn't find any other tracks, no footprints or anything, so I figured it was your cousin or his cowboys. I *did* come across several old shacks though, one of them had a dilapidated corral still standing, didn't look like anyone had been there in a long time."

"Line shacks," she nodded. "During my great-grandfather's time, they did everything on horseback. When they checked fences or branded cattle, they were away from home days at a time, so they stayed in the line shacks, and they were a god-send in the winter if someone got caught out here." At his questioning look, she explained, "During a blizzard, they could hole up in the cabin for several days. The cabins were always stocked with firewood, blankets and canned goods. If you had to use the supplies, you always replaced them later for the next person coming along."

"These shacks I found didn't have anything in them but lots of dirt and slithery critters!"

"No one stays in them anymore. We mostly check herds in our vehicles—Dean has a plane, and so do some of the other ranchers, so they can check their whole ranch in a day. But I like to ride out here on Blaze, the solitude is marvelous for one's soul." They fell into a companionable conversation, and by the time they reached his Jeep, she felt comfortable with him. Settled on the ground in the shade of the vehicle, they slaked their thirst and Bryce ate while they talked about how different life was here, compared to his in St. Louis. From his conversation, she pegged him as a harmless playboy.

"Well, as much as I enjoy your company, I better get moving," he said at last. They rose to their feet and Dorine wiped the dust off the back of her jeans as she snagged her hat off the Jeep's mirror. "You know, I didn't think I'd like it out here in the wild west...but this assignment is looking better all the time..." He let his voice trail off.

A soft burring noise startled them. "My cell phone," Dorine gestured, and whistled softly. Blaze immediately raised his head, grass sticking out of his mouth as he chewed and trotted toward her. Bryce took a step back as the horse came near and Dorine patted his velvety nose. He nuzzled her hand and whickered softly. Reaching into the backpack, she took the phone out. " Hi...yes, I'm fine...all right. No, I'm on my way back now...bye."

"Someone checking up on you?" Bryce murmured, standing with his legs apart, thumbs hooked in his belt loops and his hat shoved back, trying hard to look as western macho as he could.

Dorine tried not to grin as she shut the phone off, dropped it back in the bag and swung easily into the saddle. Leather creaked as she gathered the reins. "Dean's mother. She's always worrying about me, she's such a dear soul."

Bryce moved next to the horse, squinting up at her. "Look, I don't want to tell you your business, but I don't think it's a good idea for you to be out here by yourself."

She looked down at him, her expression hidden by the shadow of the hat brim. "I've been riding these ridges and grasslands almost since I could walk." *Did he and Dean fall out of the same mold?*

He laid a hand on her leg. "I know, but we don't really know what we're dealing with here, and it's better to be safe than sorry."

She realized he was only thinking of her safety and nodded, but didn't like the familiar way in which he touched her. "I'll be careful." *But no one is going to tell me where I can ride!*

He didn't move his hand. "By the way, can I see you again? Not about this. For dinner and a movie maybe?" Dorine's eyes twinkled. *This guy didn't waste any time!* She'd met his kind at college and had early on learned how to deal with them. "That is, unless you're seeing someone?"

She hesitated. She didn't really have any excuse not to date him. "No, there's no one special." *Oh yeah? What about that kiss last night? What about the way your nerves quiver every time Dean comes near you?* She tossed her head. "Yes, I'd like that."

"Good! I'll be in touch." He smiled with practiced charm.

*Such straight, even white teeth...but a hunk?—I don't think so, Robin!* She turned Blaze's head toward the trail. "See you!" she waggled her fingers over her shoulder and urged Blaze forward.

Bryce waved, standing there until she was out of sight. *This could turn out to be a very interesting summer!*

Even though meeting Bryce was a pleasant distraction, Dorine's thoughts returned to Dean as soon as the handsome insurance investigator was out of sight. The familiar burden on her heart weighed heavy as she remembered Dean's earlier aloofness. *Lord, is this attraction to him part of Your plan for me? Has it always been there and I haven't seen it because he's been so domineering?* Her eyes filled with tears as she prayed for the man who was becoming the foremost concern in her heart.

The house was deserted when she returned. Changing into her swimsuit, she did a few laps in the pool before pulling herself out and stretching out on a lounger. Closing her eyes, she should have felt contentment, but all she could see was Dean's tanned image, his blue eyes, and that wayward curl over his forehead that she always wanted to reach up and brush back. She wondered where he was...in Rapid with that redhead? Or somewhere else *with* someone else? Her heart turned over at that thought—no one had ever mentioned any connection with someone specific except for Darrell's reference to the redhead—*was* Dean involved with anyone? But...but...how could he have kissed her like he did, if there was someone else in the picture?!! All of a sudden, she cared very much if he was involved with another woman! When the gentle jingle of the bracelet on her arm reminded her of the giver, she touched it gently and smiled.

# CHAPTER TEN

Dorine began rising earlier than usual to ride Blaze unseen through her pastures, feeling a certain satisfaction that she had control over at least this small part of her life. However, she was very careful not to be late to work at the Double D office.

Dean had gradually added more to her workload, responsibilities that brought her into more personal contact with the business. The move puzzled her, but she accepted it with a shrug, thankful she had a good-paying job; she'd need quite a bankroll to get started on her future plans at the Circle A.

Today, Dean was out on the range with his men, moving cattle to another section. Darrell was working with the veterinarian in the barn, and the rest of the hands were hauling hay bales into storage sheds. It was another blistering hot day, the sun beating down on the parched earth with a few puffy clouds floating in the azure blue overhead.

Dorine glanced up when the office door opened, admitting a map-laden Bryce, paper rolls tucked under his arm. He was in a business suit today instead of western wear, with carefully groomed hair and she speculated that he *could* be considered a hunk…?

He gave her an engaging smile when he spotted her, greeted Hazel, Loretta and Emily in a flirty, well-practiced manner.

"Hi there, Bryce!" Hazel noted his lingering glance at Dorine. "Dorine tells me she met you out on the range last week."

"She thought I was an outlaw," he teased in a voice meant to be seductive as he gave Dorine another one of those flirty looks.

"Stranger things have happened," Dorine retorted. How come he couldn't tell his manner left her cold?

He laughed, then turned to Hazel. "I wanted to show Dean these maps—is he anywhere around?"

"Not at the moment, but if you wanted to leave them, come on in here," she replied.

"Dorine," he turned to her, "this concerns your land too, so if you want to look, come on." She rose and followed him behind Hazel through double doors that opened into the conference room. Switching on overhead lights, Hazel indicated that Bryce should spread his paperwork on the large conference table.

Not only were DeFoe Enterprise meetings held here, but Dean was generous in opening the room for cattlemen's meetings and seminars, 4-H club gatherings and other conferences. Large picture windows looked north over rippling grasslands, with the barns in the foreground and the arena to the right. Book shelves lined another wall, while a third wall held enlarged pictures of the various DeFoe businesses.

Bryce laid out the maps while Dorine got several heavy volumes off the shelves to hold down the unruly corners. Bryce took that opportunity to sweep his gaze over her trim figure, admiring her slender legs and graceful movements. She was in a skirt and blouse today, looking cool and professional. He wondered what she'd look like in a bikini.

The phone rang in the outer office and Loretta called for Hazel. Left alone, Bryce began pointing out features on the map, aware of the attractive young woman beside him. This was business, after all. *Yeah, right.*

When he'd finished, Dorine smiled, turning to lead the way to the outer office. "Thanks for bringing these, Dean will look them over when he gets back." His nearness didn't cause one skip in her heart beat. *A hunk? Maybe to you, Robin!* "You're not driving the Jeep?"

He laughed, a nice-sounding masculine laugh. "No, today is more white shirt and tie day," he glanced down at his attire. "Besides, I don't want to be out there so much that the rustlers get spooked at seeing the same vehicle traveling around and get suspicious."

They stepped into the office and Dorine leaned against her desk, a worried frown on her face. "Have you seen anybody that looks suspicious? We recognize everyone around here in a 20-mile radius, and we'd know it if someone strange was poking around."

He glanced uneasily at the other secretaries but then realized they probably knew what was going on anyway—after all, this was ranch country and everyone would be as concerned as the DeFoes were. "These—crooks, rustlers, whatever—use modern-day technology. We've found they stake out an area for weeks or even months before they move in. With helicopters, trucks and high-powered binoculars, they can move in and out of an area so fast it would make your head spin. Then they go underground again." He looked at his watch. "It's close to noon, I can tell you more about this over lunch...where should we go to eat?"

Dorine's lips twitched at the man's conceit, assuming that she'd jump at the chance to be with him, but she could never bring herself to be rude or unkind to anyone. Besides, lunch with Bryce might take her mind off one tall, rugged rancher. "We can just run into Silverdale. My best friend Robin, owns the Sweet Schoppe—so we'll get plenty to eat!" She slid the desk drawer open to grab her purse.

Bryce eagerly opened the exit door with a flourish, winked at an astonished Loretta and Emily, managing to brush his hand over Dorine's back at the same time. For just an instant, she wondered if this was a mistake. Dean's aloofness popped into her mind and she squared her shoulders and lifted her chin. By golly, she'd enjoy this lunch if it killed her!

Hazel watched the two young people leave with mixed emotions. Bryce was nice enough, but she wondered what Dean would think of his little gal keeping company with the city feller? She glanced at Loretta and Emily, who quickly busied themselves. They normally didn't gossip but just like herself, they were probably wondering why Dorine would want to date Bryce, when Dean was right here?

Hazel's husband of 30 years always told her that when you couldn't admire the opposite sex's attractions, you might as well be dead. And Dean was a "hunk," like modern girls said, both he and Darrell. She knew that although Loretta and Emily were happily married, they couldn't hide the admiration when they looked at either of the DeFoe brothers...so why was Dorine so blind?!!

Bryce entertained Dorine all the way into town with stories that had a more humorous side, and she found him a pleasant companion.

They walked into the Sweet Schoppe, crowded with regulars, and a hush descended. For the first time she could remember, Dorine felt uncomfortable under the curious glances as she led Bryce to a table. Conversation gradually resumed but she realized she and Bryce were the subject of subdued remarks. Robin raised a questioning eyebrow when she brought water to their table and asked for their order. Dorine glanced up at Robin's brusque tone and felt her neck and cheeks grow warm. She knew now that coming here with Bryce had been a mistake—everyone in the café knew it and Robin didn't bother to hide her displeasure.

After they'd ordered and Robin hurried off to the kitchen, Bryce eyed Dorine. "I thought you said she was your best friend—what was *that* about?" He gazed after the little redhead. She was a plump armful but still kinda cute—however, the wedding band told him she was off-limits.

Dorine recognized his predatory expression as he followed Robin's progress and realized that any woman who took his glib compliments seriously was asking for trouble. She relaxed, knowing he wasn't a threat to her. When he finally looked back at her, she grinned. "We'd never need a newspaper in Silverdale—a person can't do anything or go anywhere around this country. News seems to... float in the air," she waved her hand to encompass the room.

"So?" he looked perplexed.

"Robin, and everyone else in here, thinks I'm being disloyal to a...ah...a *friend*, by letting you take me out to lunch; in fact, people here would say it's a date."

He studied her until she looked away. "So....this has something to do with one of the DeFoes, doesn't it?" he asked shrewdly.

"She seems to think so!" Dorine nodded towards her friend.

Bryce glanced around at the covert looks they were getting and whispered, "I don't think she's the only one."

Dorine's eyes traveled over the room. "They're just curious because you're a stranger. Remember when I told you I knew everyone in a 20-mile radius?" Tipping her head towards the room in general, she added gently, "They're the same way."

Robin brought their plates at that moment, slapping the bill on the table. The steaming meal was as delicious as it smelled, but Dorine had lost her appetite. Bryce, however, dug in, ignoring looks from the townspeople, until they returned their attention to their own meals. *This little Robin gal could really cook!* And, *he* loved to eat. He'd been here several times during the past month, just to grab a quick sandwich, but had only glimpsed Robin in the back. He'd never tasted her popular, homemade hearty meals.

After they'd eaten, Bryce leaned forward, propping his elbows on the table. "Have you ever thought about getting out of here?"

Dorine gazed at him with puzzlement as she carefully laid her knife across the edge of her plate. "Getting out of here? You mean leave the ranch?" At his nod, she stared hard at him. "Why would I want to do that? This is home, the only place I'll ever want to be."

He held her gaze. "What's holding you here?"

"My roots—I have no desire to go elsewhere."

"But you saw a whole different side of life when you went to college—didn't you realize how…how restrictive this life is?"

"Bryce, this isn't the Wild West anymore—we even have indoor privies!" She relented at his chagrined expression. "You won't find too many young ranchers nowadays *without* a college degree."

"Didn't that other way of life interest you even a little?"

She shook her head, searching his eyes. "What are you getting at?"

He shrugged, glancing around then back to her. "You're a very attractive woman, come-hither eyes, gorgeous hair, and a killer figure—you could easily make it as a high class model."

She felt the blush creeping up her neck, coloring her cheeks. "I wouldn't want that kind of life."

"But you haven't even *seen* the world, you have *no idea* of what's out there!" he insisted.

She smiled and patted his hand. "On both counts, you're wrong—I've been all over Europe and, one of my college roommates was a model."

That didn't deter him. "You're just burying yourself out here in this God-forsaken place—"

Her hand on his arm stopped him. "First of all, Bryce, God has never forsaken any of His creation, and secondly, this is where I believe He wants me."

He leaned back, a cynical gleam in his eye. "Don't tell me you're one of those Bible-thumpers," he drawled sarcastically.

"If that's what you want to call it," she replied softly, a serene expression on her face. "Jesus means everything to me."

He sighed, a resigned look replacing the cynicism as he shook his head and muttered something that sounded like "What a waste." He picked up the bill but by the time they went out the door, his good humor was restored. "Boy, you could have cut the air in there with a knife!" he laughed, draping an unwelcome arm over her shoulder.

Dorine edged away. "We should've gone some place else, where they wouldn't have known us!"

Bryce laughed heartily as he unlocked the car door.

"Who did you think was going to steal your car?" Dorine teased. They looked around at the deserted, sun-drenched street. He grinned, shrugged and helped her in. As she fastened her seat belt, she realized Bryce could only ever be just enjoyable company, nothing more. She'd have to make sure *Robin* realized it too!

When they drove in the yard, Darrell was ambling towards the barn, a toothpick dangling out of one corner of his mouth. "Well, did you enjoy your lunch?" he asked pleasantly, but Dorine detected an under-lying sarcasm, totally foreign to his personality. He stopped beside the car, resting his hands on his hips and looking so much like Dean that Dorine was startled. She got out, eyeing his challenging stance. *Not him too*! She lifted her chin a little higher. "Yes, as a matter of fact, we did!" She slammed the door harder than necessary.

"Mrs. Mac was wondering when you were coming to eat," Darrell drawled, glancing from Dorine to Bryce.

Dorine slapped one hand over her mouth. "Ohmygosh! I forgot to tell her that I wouldn't be here today!"

Darrell nodded knowingly. "There's still some pie left." Bryce was eyeing him closely. Something was going on here, and his male instincts were on the alert. Was this his competition for Dorine?

"I'll have to go smooth her feathers," Dorine said hurriedly, then trotting backwards, she waved at Bryce. "Thanks for the lunch and I'll see you later." His appreciative gaze followed her out of sight.

The two men sized each other up in the ensuing silence. Bryce spoke first. "I guess I've stepped on somebody's toes," he remarked sheepishly, then shrugged. "But she *said* she wasn't seeing anyone..."

Darrell shook his head, working the toothpick around to the corner of his mouth, seeming to enjoy the other man's discomfort. "It isn't me," he finally chuckled, leaning against the car and crossing his arms over his chest. "Thank God!" he shuddered comically.

Bryce stared at him. "You don't mean it's *Dean*?!!"

Darrell held back a smile as he nodded.

"Of *course* it's Dean," Bryce answered his own question. "Why not? Who could compete with the All American Cowboy?" he continued, but without rancor. Glancing at the house, he frowned. "Why didn't she say anything?" He ran his hand over his hair.

"'Cause she doesn't know it yet herself," Darrell replied. "We've grown up together," he explained, "and she's always thought of us as brothers...but I don't think Dean has considered her a 'kid sister' for a l-o-n-g time! Since she got home from college, you ought to see the fireworks!" An understanding expression slid over Bryce's face and he shook his head, grinning to himself.

Darrell liked Bryce. "Come on, let's go see about getting some of that pie!" He clapped the shorter man on the shoulder and they walked companionably to the house, passing Dorine as she hurried back to the office, sparing them only a fleeting smile.

Dean came into the office later that afternoon, slapping the dust off his hat before he stepped through the door. He looked tired and dusty, with animal hair clinging to his jeans as he crossed to the washroom. Dorine followed him with her eyes, thinking of how different he appeared now that she thought of him as...as what? An attractive man? The confusion assailed her again—Dean would no longer be her friend, her comforter—that man was gone forever, that much she knew…their relationship had subtly changed over that past few weeks and she felt like she was floundering in a sea of emotion. Glad that her work required her complete attention, she buried herself in it.

When Dean returned, he gave Dorine a quick wink before going into his office. Her heart thudded, a warmth spreading through her. She wished she was more of a sophisticate—but she wasn't, she could only be who she was, a forthright, small-town girl.

"Hazel," Dean came out of the office later with the bundle of letters in his hand, "I'd really like these to go out in today's mail. Why don't you knock off early to get them to the post office?"

"Oh," Hazel looked uncertain, "I wasn't going to go that way…but Dorine could take them, couldn't you, hon?" Dorine nodded and reached for the bundle, carefully controlling her reaction when her fingers brushed Dean's. He smiled and gave her an outrageous wink before turning back to his office. She found it hard to breathe when he was in her space and was glad to hurry out to her car.

Slipping the bundle of letters into the slot at the post office, she passed the time of day with Mrs. Kingston before walking on down the dusty street to the Sweet Schoppe. Dark clouds covered the late afternoon sun, and thunder rumbled in the distance. They could really use a good soaking rain, but so far, there were just scattered showers here and there. Robin was busy in the kitchen, but grinned and raised a spatula in response to Dorine's greeting. Her face a rosy hue from the grill, Robin said, "Oh, my aching feet! This heat is murder!"

Dorine eyed her suspiciously. "You're not pregnant again, are you?"

"No, no chance of that," smiled Robin, fanning herself. "Randy hasn't been home lately." She laughed at her own joke before noticing Dorine had given her only a token smile. She studied her friend's face. "You got something on your mind? Not that insurance guy, I hope!"

Dorine glanced away. "Robin." She sighed. "It was only lunch."

She absently fingered her bracelet, then looked back at her friend. "And that's all it could *ever* be...I don't find him 'hunky'!"

Robin laughed as she kept stirring a large pan of gravy, her glance flitting to Dorine's troubled look. "Wanna tell me about it?"

"It's kind of complicated...something has changed between Dean and I." She twisted the braid end in her fingers, tilting her head.

"Let me get this served up, then we'll talk—Jamie!" Robin called to the teen waitress, quickly got her customer served and came back to pull up another stool, waiting expectantly.

"I can't explain it," Dorine sent her friend a miserable look. "My feelings are...different...towards him."

"Different how?"

Dorine shrugged, her cheeks pink. "I hate to admit it, but I think...I think I'm....starting to...*like* him." She wouldn't look at Robin. "Ever since he kissed me the other night."

Robin's eyebrows went up, a gleeful expression in her eyes. "Did you kiss him back?!!"

"Of course not! Well...I don't know...yes, I did! Satisfied?!!"

Cupping her hands around her mug, Robin leaned forward, her eyes sparkling. "Is he a good kisser?"

Dorine's cheeks colored a brighter pink. "Ro-bin!"

"Well, is he?"

"You just don't quit, do you?" she laughed self-consciously. "I have to admit...my toes *did* curl...and stop your laughing!"

Robin tried valiantly to hold in her laughter but it spilled out. "Oh, Dorine, you ought to see yourself. You don't have a clue, do you?!"

"What do you mean?!!"

Robin leaned forward. "You're attracted to him!"

"No!" Dorine shook her head violently. "To *him*?!! Never!!"

"Dorine, listen," Robin sobered, her hand on Dorine's arm. "You're not the same gal that left here a few years ago, and people change. You've matured and you're finally seeing Dean as an attractive *man*!"

"But..."

"No buts, even you have to admit he's a hunk!"

"Wel-l-l, yes," Dorine conceded, the image of Dean's undeniable masculinity springing to mind.

"Any of the single women in this county, and, even some of the *married* ones, would give their eyeteeth to get his attention!" Robin got up to refill her cup. "And you, my dear, have had his attention for a long-g-g time!" At Dorine's skeptical look, Robin laughed. "Haven't you ever wondered how come he hasn't married by now? Most men around here are married by the time they're his age."

"Clint isn't, neither is Deputy Langley and a couple of the Anderson guys—"

Robin waved her hand dismissively. "Sure there's a few, but what I'm getting at, is, did it ever occur to you that he's been waiting…waiting for *you*?"

"No, it hasn't!" Dorine replied flatly. "All he sees in me is someone to boss around and control. Besides, the day after he kissed me, he acted like I had the pox."

"Maybe you scared him off," Robin mused, tilting her head.

"He could just as well have put a sign around his neck, 'Do not touch'."

Customers came in, the little bell above the door jangling merrily. "We need to talk about this some more. You haven't eaten yet, why don't you stay for supper? Call Marci," Robin commanded as she slid off the stool. Dorine hesitated for only a moment, then reached for the phone. She really did need to talk to someone!

After closing up and cleaning the kitchen, Robin and Dorine stepped through the connecting door from the café into the attached apartment, where Jason and Jeremy exuberantly greeted their mother. The neighbor girl that had been watching them let herself out the back door after greeting Dorine. When the little boys shyly came to give her hugs, their affection tugged at her heart. If she could feel this way about someone else's children, how much more would she feel about her own?

After the boys were in bed, Robin listened to Dorine pour out her heart, silently inviting her confidence as she always had. Her eyes softened. "Dorine? Look at me." When Dorine reluctantly raised her eyes, Robin nodded sweetly. "You're in love."

"No! I don't *want* to love him!" Dorine sprang up from the sofa and began pacing. "This isn't happening, I've got things I want to do, and he's always trying to…to….*dominate* me," she stopped abruptly and her anger suddenly died as she looked helplessly at Robin. "Do you really think I am?" Her arms flopped to her side.

Robin nodded and laughed with delight, clapping her hands. "I was wondering when you'd catch on! He's been in love with you *forever*! I've watched the way he looked at you when he didn't think you'd catch him looking."

Dorine's knees went weak and she dropped on the sofa beside her friend. Shaking her head, she blurted out, "Well, why doesn't he just *say* something? Instead of keeping me on a string…like a yo-yo! Besides, he's got girlfriends, Darrell even said so."

"Of course he's got girl *friends*, he's not exactly ugly, but…" she hesitated, "have you ever given him the *chance* to say anything?"

Dorine was silent, holding her hand over her eyes, then raised her head and looked at Robin. "No, I guess I haven't…but," she sputtered, "I *can't* be in love with him—most of the time, *I don't even like him*!"

"Sometimes, that's the way love feels," Robin replied. "Randy and I had our squabbles too, but nothing like *you* guys! As soon as we laid eyes on each other, we knew we'd be together—and we *told* each other! It seemed like we were always in tune with each other's thoughts…but it sounds like you and Dean *never* agree on *anything*! I don't know if I could offer you any advice or not, but, we know that God is in control, in spite of us trying to help Him."

Dorine smiled sadly and laid her hand on Robin's where it rested on the sofa between them. "I'll just have to take it day by day. I don't know enough about romance to put in a pig's eye."

"Just be your sweet self, Dorine, and go with your feelings. But, we need to enlist Bigger Guns about this!" Her eyes twinkled before reaching for Dorine's hand. As she lifted their hearts to heaven requesting God's guidance, Dorine felt once again the Presence of God, surrounding her with His love and comfort.

# CHAPTER ELEVEN

There was so much to learn about the transportation of the rough stock to various rodeos that Dorine seldom had time to dwell on her changing feelings towards Dean, but he was never far from her thoughts. She immersed herself in handling travel arrangements, checking on transports, drivers and insurances and all the problems that cropped up, shutting him out when he intruded too much.

People came and went, and there were meetings scheduled both here and away, which had Dean putting in a lot of travel time. In a way, Dorine was glad that he wasn't in the office every day, she didn't have to hide her growing feelings—but when he was gone, life lost its sparkle. When he *was* there, he let her know firmly that he expected her to sit in on meetings with Hazel so she could familiarize herself with proceedings. This side of him was puzzling... unless? Was this his way of apologizing for his abrupt dismissal of her guest ranch plans? Was he helping to familiarize herself with business dealings to run the guest ranch? A warm glow spread through her as she had to acknowledge his kindness and thoughtfulness. Bit by bit, she realized, he was endearing himself to her. And what was she going to do about it?

However, one of the biggest surprises at the meetings was Darrell—he was thoughtful, serious and profound in discussions, and she was gratified to see that Dean often yielded the floor to his younger brother. Darrell's sense of humor had often led people to think that he didn't have a serious thought in his head, but that humor masked a shrewd mind, one even she didn't see very often.

But for her, there was only one interesting man at those meetings—and she could openly observe Dean as he conducted the proceedings. He was a good communicator, listening to others' ideas, then outlining plans that indicated thoughtful consideration. Slowly, over time, her opinion of him grew more positive as she watched him interact tactfully with difficult people. She began to doubt the image of him she'd had all these years. *Had* he only been trying to help her, guide her? She played back in her mind some of their previous arguments, such as the one on her college graduation morning—

"Dorine?"

His voice jerked her back to the meeting at hand, and she saw everyone had turned toward her expectantly.

"I-I'm sorry, I was….wool gathering," she flustered, grabbing at the first explanation that came to mind, a warmth creeping up her neck.

"In front of all these *cattlemen*?!!" Dean grinned while the room erupted into good-natured laughter.

Thinking fast, she quipped, "We-l-l, you can shear sheep and get something to wear, whereas with cattle….?" She let her voice trail off and glanced flirtatiously up at him as the room erupted in laughter again.

He winked as he leaned close. "You're pretty fast on the draw there, pardner!" Then he grew serious and tapped the paper in front of her. "I was asking about the figures on the rodeo contracts from last month." He was secretly delighted with her quick comeback and wished he could wrap his arms around her and—but he had to stop fantasizing, especially during this meeting!

Dorine tossed the room in general a saucy grin and read off the figures. People took notes and the conversation moved on. When the meeting ended, she and Hazel went straight to their computers to compile information, and groups of people drifted out into the office towards the door. Dean caught her watching for him and raised his eyebrow before giving her a sly wink. She jerked her eyes back to the screen, heat suffusing her cheeks. When she glanced up again, he was just going out the door and she sighed in relief that he was gone for the time being. How could she ever getting anything done with him around?!!

However, she wouldn't have been so glad he was gone, if she'd known where Dean was heading after he'd seen his guests off.

When he drove into the rest stop off the freeway, Bryce was there, leaning against the side of his Jeep. Dean parked and got out of his pickup, pulling his hat lower over his eyes as he ambled towards the shorter man. After a brief greeting, Bryce informed him that it was almost certain Alfred was mixed up in a rustling ring that had been operating all over western South Dakota.

Tight-lipped, Dean crossed his arms over his chest and leaned against the Jeep, studying the ground at his crossed feet. Bryce mentioned that aerial photos could be taken from Dean's plane, as he frequently flew over the area and wouldn't arouse any suspicions since the rustlers had probably seen the plane before. He turned and opened the door of the Jeep, pulling out a packet of maps and spreading some on the hood. Glancing quickly around, he scanned the few cars that were parked under shade trees, his sharp gaze assessing tourists who were stretching their legs.

Dean's eyes mirrored amusement as he held down one corner of the map to keep it from blowing away. "You suspect any of them?"

"Never can be too sure of anything in this business," Bryce replied.

As they were studying the maps, Dean casually said, "I heard about your lunch with Dorine." He paused before adding, "She's off-limits." He kept his eyes on the map.

"You heard about that? Of *course* you did, Darrell's your brother."

Dean turned sideways, pinning the shorter man with his intense gaze. "He doesn't carry tales—but don't ask her out again."

Bryce studied the unsmiling rancher whose tenseness radiated from him. He'd rather have him as a friend than not. Placing a hand over his heart in a dramatic pose, Bryce exclaimed pitifully, "Better a broken heart than a broken arm or leg!"

Dean relaxed, his lips twitching. "Show me what we've got here."

Bryce's eyes twinkled but he followed Dean's lead, plunging into the seriousness of their mutual problem.

Dean drove slowly back to the ranch, mulling over their discussion. This was a particularly clever bunch of rustlers, operating at random so there was no pattern to their movements. He rested his elbow on the window, rubbing his fingers over his chin. His eyes wandered over the landscape where heat waves shimmered up from the ground. It was another blistering day, and he needed to check the water pumps in one of the pastures. Soon his mind skipped from the rustlers to Dorine—if she *did* have a hankering for the insurance investigator, he hoped he'd nipped *that* in the bud!

Many weekends, the brothers were gone to rodeos, either as stock contractors or competitors; sometimes they were gone almost a week. Dorine tried to hide her wistfulness as they left each time, but realized she wasn't in a position to rodeo...perhaps next summer, when all these bizarre happenings were solved.

The one bright spot was seeing Dean attending church, but she suspected it was because of appearances, not any desire on his part to get close to God. She caught herself watching his face one morning, as a muscle worked in his jaw during the sermon—was he having disturbing thoughts? She certainly hoped so, and intensified her prayers on his behalf.

She would occasionally drive over to her own ranch office, since it made Marci nervous for Dorine to ride her horse. She stayed away from the house, but went to the tack room/office to look through the mail that Alfred now left on the desk for her.

One day while she was reconciling the bank statement, it occurred to her how contented she felt. Familiar odors of leather, horse and hay from the tack room surrounded her like old friends, and dust motes danced in a shaft of sunlight streaming in through the window. The sound of a tractor droning somewhere in the distance added to her contentment, topped off with a symphony from the birds twittering as they dipped and glided in the field beyond the open door.

Sudden thoughts of the rustlers sliced into her contentment and the silence now took on an uneasiness air. She raised her head and looked out. It was pleasant, not sweltering like it had been, with white puffy clouds floating in the azure sky. Flies buzzed lazily, and for once, not even a breeze was stirring. She stood and went to the door. Every sound she made was amplified—she could even hear her own breathing. A sense of loss assailed her, a loss of innocence and trust because of the rustlers. Where were they today? Were they strangers? Or did they walk the streets of Silverdale in daylight and prowl their neighbors' pastures at night?

Off in the distance, dust rose lazily from the fields, and she felt better knowing the ranch hands were working close by. She went back to the desk, but the silence still bothered her.

After she'd reconciled the statement, she went to the garden shed and took out the hose to water the flowers on the north side of the house. She watched the sprinkler arc water overhead and was just enjoying the beautiful rainbow the spray created, when there was a noise behind her. She whirled around.

Alfred stood there, a scowl on his face. She put her hand over her heart, breathing deeply. "Alfred! You scared the dickens out of me!"

"Saw ya come a while ago, and thought I'd check to see if ya was alright." He squinted at her uncertainly, looking at the hose then back at her. "I been keepin' everythin' watered," he added defensively. "Thought you was workin' full-time for DeFoe?"

"You thought right. I got done early today and came over to catch up on bookwork. I know you're busy too, so thought I'd save you some time by doing this." *And besides, why should I have to defend myself to you?*

"Doesn't take long to turn on a sprinkler and let it run."

He didn't want her to water the lawn. But why? "Alfred, my mother planted all this and it gives me pleasure to care for it....it's something I can do for her memory, she enjoyed them so much."

He didn't say anything, standing first on one foot and then the other. "Wall-l-l, jest wanted ya to know that I been doin' my job...besides," he took his hat off and resettled it on his head, "wouldn't want nothin' to happen to ya."

"Thanks for worrying about me, Alfred, but do you really think the vandals or rustlers, or whatever they are, are still around here? We haven't heard anything for awhile now."

"Jest the same, I kinda wish ya wouldn't come over here."

"I'll be alright, Alfred," she said soothingly, turning to move the hose. When she glanced behind her, he was heading for the barn, shaking his head.

She couldn't worry about smoothing his ruffled feathers, she had work to do. Eyeing the weeds by the sheds, she went to get the scythe. Chopping down the undesirable overgrowth gave her an immense feeling of satisfaction she decided a half hour later, stopping to wipe her brow. Feeling thirsty, she walked over to the lawn and picked up the hose. She allowed the water to rinse her face, feeling refreshed and—a shadow fell over her. She yelped and dropped the hose, her heart thundering as she looked up. "Bryce!"

He didn't smile. "What are you doing here?"

"Do you make a *habit* of just *popping* up out of nowhere?!" She swiped at the water on her face, embarrassed at her appearance.

"How come you're here?" His face was stern, his brown eyes stormy. No longer the "hunk," he was pure investigator.

"Bryce, I know you mean well, but this *is* my home, and I have every right to be here." She brushed aside the twinge of guilt, disregarding the promise she'd made Dean.

"Didn't DeFoe tell you how dangerous it is to come around here?" Bryce's eyes remained cold and hard.

"Well, he's always wanting me to carry the cell phone—"

"What good is it if you can't get to it? Look how both Alfred and I surprised you." He quickly shot down her defense.

"You saw him?" Dorine squeaked out.

He nodded, scowling at her. "Look, I know how anxious you are to get back into your house, but you could be putting yourself in danger." He rested his hands on his hips, the scowl deepening.

She stared back at him. "I doubt that. Vandals wouldn't come around if they know someone is here, and rustlers work in the dark, at night, don't they?" she replied with a challenging lift of her chin.

He tilted his head and studied her as though debating how to answer, then shook his head. "I don't know why you're being so stubborn about this—"

"I don't like being ordered around on my own property!" He saw her chin come up even more and had to suppress a grin. DeFoe had told him about her strong will. When he didn't answer, she threw her hands up in the air and stepped away from him. "I've already promised Dean I wouldn't be here without someone close by," she turned and waved a hand in the direction of the fields, "and you can see the ranch hands are working right over there."

She turned back to catch him regarding her solemnly. "I just don't want anything to happen to you," he said quietly. The second time she'd heard that today.

"I can take care of myself," she replied more gently, then added softly, "but thanks for your concern."

He shook his head, dropping his hands. "Just keep your wits about you, okay?" She nodded as he walked towards the barn, disappearing around the corner....and, she'd just lost her gardening enthusiasm. The weeds would have to wait until another day.

Returning to Defoes, Dorine never mentioned the incident to anyone, hoping Bryce wouldn't either—or Dean would have her hide!

However, there were several letters for her that wiped it from her mind. One was a thick packet of graduation day photographs sent by her former roommate, after Dorine had written to let her know where she was staying.

Leaning against the kitchen counter, she showed the photographs to Marci and Mrs. Mac. "Look at this one!" She was laughing delightedly when Dean came into the kitchen. He eyed the pictures as he went to the refrigerator for a glass of ice water, turning to watch Dorine's animated face, aglow with fond memories.

As she looked at the pose of herself in front of her dorm, she murmured, "And just think, all this was possible because of that trust fund my dad left for me—" She broke off and looked up when Dean choked and began coughing, quickly setting down his glass.

"Mercy, son! Did you swallow wrong?" Marci quickly got up and went to him, slapping him on the back.

"I'm okay," he finally managed to get out, wiping moisture from his eyes. "Just swallowed down my Sunday pipe!" He threw a sharp look at Dorine, turned and strode out of the room, still clearing his throat. *Would the secret he carried drive her from him, once she knew?*

"I used to get so scared when they were little and would choke like that, and I'm still the same way!" Marci declared, sitting back down.

"It's scary no matter how old they are," agreed Mrs. Mac.

Dorine nodded absently, thinking of that strange glance he had directed at her—was he thinking of their argument on graduation morning? She felt her face flush as she recalled her harsh words, and turned her attention to her other letters.

Marci had opened a large envelope, her eyes widening in excitement. "Look here, gals! These are the new designs Darcy has made up for her line of clothing at the western store!" Dorine and Mrs. Mac crowded around to see how the artistic Darcy had applied her talent to creating a new line of western wear for women and children. Once in production, they would be carried at all the stores in the chain that DeFoe Enterprises owned. Dorine could see the pride that Marci had in her only daughter and was glad she could be here to witness the success of "D-D's Duds."

One morning after breakfast, Dean stuck his head in the door. "Dorine, are you ready to repair fences today?" He had mentioned previously that they needed to restring a section of wire in their mutual boundary fence. "I want to get started before it gets too hot." His eyes ran approvingly over her jeans and work shirt, causing a flush to creep up her neck. *How could just a look from him do that to her?!!*

However, she managed to answer calmly, "Okay, be right there." Quickly finishing the folding of her laundry, she ran lightly up the stairs to put it away. Filling her water bottle, she grabbed her sunglasses and heavy work gloves, lifting her straw hat off the peg as she went out.

Dean was throwing tools into the bed of the old ranch pickup when she arrived at the barn and she gritted her teeth at seeing his glance at her gloves before they got in. Still checking on her like she was a child! She fumed silently as he started the pickup, shifting gears when he came to the first gate. Without hesitation, she pulled on her gloves as she got out, shoving the door shut behind her. It was an unwritten rule that passengers, male or female, opened gates while out on the range.

He asked her questions about a current rodeo contract and she gradually relaxed on the ride to the pasture. Once, he silently pointed to a family of deer, heads raised, bodies quivering for flight.

Dorine smiled at the sight, turning to Dean only to find him watching her instead of the deer. She was intensely aware of him, of how close they were, how secluded. They gazed at each other and time stood still, the silence broken only by the call of a meadowlark, and a soft, fresh breeze stirring the prairie grass.

At that moment, she realized she'd never want to be anywhere else but here in South Dakota, next to this strong, protective man who was so sensitive to his surroundings. But was it because of their long-standing friendship, or was it something bigger, stronger?

The spell was broken when he abruptly turned away and drove on. She took a deep breath to steady her nerves and realized she'd have to be more careful to school her expression to blandness and be hidden from his inscrutable gaze.

They topped a rise and Dean stopped in a swirl of dust that was whipped away by the ever-present Dakota breeze—just like her turbulent emotions where whipped around by his changing moods. He got out and slammed the door, heading to the rear of the pickup. Dorine joined him, reaching for the tools. He tipped his head to indicate the direction they'd take. "That looks like a weak post down there." She grabbed the shovel while he hoisted a pole over his shoulder and they made their way down the slope.

They worked easily together, each knowing what the other needed. In the light of their differences, she marveled at how well they worked as one. She jumped when he abruptly asked, "Do you have plans for the future, other than the guest ranch?" He didn't look at her as he dumped a shovelful of dirt to the side of the hole.

"Just getting the guest business up and running is going to take a lot of my time…is that what you mean?"

"Sort of." He turned to look at her. Trickles of sweat made their way down the side of his tanned face. "I was thinking more along the lines of your personal life…"

She tensed. "It really isn't any of your business but are you asking if there's someone important, like a 'significant other'?"

"You've never mentioned anyone, so how am I to know?" he replied as he put his foot on the shovel again and rammed it into the earth, then turned to toss the dirt. "You must have met lots of men in the last four years." He stopped and leaned on the shovel, watching her.

Looking away from him, she noticed a hawk soaring aloft, its graceful flight a thing of beauty. "Yes, I met a lot of people…"

"*Is* there anyone special?"

She dropped her gaze from the hawk to see the intensity in his expression. She should have let him stew for butting into her life again, but her conscience reminded her that she was no longer a giddy teen, pitting her adolescent resentment against him. It wasn't in her to play games either. She shook her head. "No, there's no one special, even though it's none of your business." She gave a deprecating little laugh and tossed her head. "Not that there weren't some who wanted to be…but they wanted more than what I was willing to give."

His face grew dark. "They didn't—"

"No," she quickly assured him. "Nothing ever happened, Dean." She realized she was gripping the pole like a lifeline, and relaxed her fingers. "I've never allowed myself to get into situations that could lead to something immoral." Then, with a shaky breath, she plunged on. "God has always been my Protection, and He's with me every moment of every day."

He was studying her with a thoughtful look and she braced herself for his usual railing against God. But he surprised her when he replied quietly, "I'm glad you have your faith, Dorine." He indicated the hole. "I think that's deep enough, you want to drop the post in?" To him, the subject was clearly closed but she knew she couldn't let this opportunity pass.

"What happened to yours, Dean? Your faith?"

He stilled, then reached down for the shovel, muscles rippling under his sweat-stained shirt. When he straightened, his face had hardened. "I don't have faith in a God who takes people before their time." He began shoveling dirt into the hole, tamping it down with his booted foot. "My dad never got to see any of us graduate from college, never got to walk Darcy down the aisle, never got to see his grandchildren—don't tell me about a caring God!" His voice grew more bitter as he threw dirt around the pole. Then he straightened, staring down at the ground, his chest heaving. Heavy silence surrounded them, broken only by the merry melody of a nearby meadowlark.

In the silence, Dorine whispered, "I lost my dad too, Dean."

He froze.

"You at least have your mother." Her words were filled with pain.

He turned, anguish filling his eyes. He dropped the shovel and took a step toward her, but she turned her face away and he stopped, his arms hanging loosely by his side. "I'm sorry, Dorine, so very sorry...I just didn't think..." his voice trailed away. He took off his glove and scrubbed his hand down over his face. "I've been so wrapped up in my loss that I've forgotten you've lost so much more." He raised his eyes and gazed at her. She was so beautiful, bathed in the sunlight, so close and yet... so far away. A wisp of dark hair escaped from her braid and blew across her face, shadowed under the brim of her western straw hat. Sliding her hand out of her work glove, she reached up to tuck the errant strand of hair behind her ear and wiped the tear away.

"I could be angry with God too, like you are, Dean, but I've learned to trust Him more through all my trouble. Everything that happens is in His plan—we can't always see that, but in the end, His plan is much better than anything I could devise. My parents are better off with Him...I could never turn my back on Him."

"Like I did." The statement wasn't the least bit apologetic.

Her gaze slid away as she looked out over the sun-drenched

rangelands. "Yes, like you did. You just up and quit trusting Him." Then her gaze swung back to him. "But God never turned His back on you, Dean. He's been there all along, waiting for you, watching over you...loving you."

Uncertainty washed over him at her simple words of faith. He absently slapped his glove against his jeans-covered thigh, looking down at the ground as though there were answers written there. A momentary envy filled him, thinking of how strong her faith was. But then the anger forced its way back into his heart and he tightened his lips. Lifting his head, he shot her a skeptical look. "I have to respect you for your views but I'll never understand how you can keep on worshiping a God that has taken everything from you!"

Her face softened and a glow filled her eyes. "He has not taken, Dean, He's given me everything—joy, peace, and His promise to not ever leave me. But best of all, I have eternal life with Him...and that comes from trusting in Him."

There was silence. "I guess that's where we differ, I don't have any joy or feel any peace...and as for His promise to not leave?" Dean yanked his glove on. "I haven't felt the presence of God in years!" He reached for the wire stretcher and grasped the end of the loose wire. "Everything good that's happened has come about because of my hard work, and Darrell's. Things haven't been any worse or any better." He yanked the wire taut and nodded towards the sturdy sack of staples. "Want to hand me one of those?"

What she *wanted* to do, was cry out in frustration, and as she fished one of the shiny new staples out of the sack, her mind whirled with scriptures to quote. "Have you ever considered that God is still blessing you, in spite of your distrust?" Dean drove the staple into the post with a few powerful smacks of the hammer.

"You're quite the little missionary, aren't you, Ms. Andrews? But you're wasting your breath, I've made up my mind." She really hated that cynical look he wore. "So let's drop it." He turned away from her before she'd found her voice.

"But Dean—"

"No more!" His voice was hard as he yanked on the next strand of wire. "The subject is closed!" She silently handed him the staples and they worked in an awkward silence. He glanced at her once, wanting to say something to soften his words, but pride reared its ugly head. He saw the wetness on her cheek and felt a prick of conscience, but his lips remained sealed. Grabbing the shovel again, he dug the next hole while she hurried to the pickup to bring back another post.

When they were done, Dean threw the tools into the pickup bed with more force than was necessary, while Dorine slid into the passenger seat. The ride back to the house was silent, as she gazed sightlessly out the window. They could as well have been on two separate continents and her heart nearly broke to have him so close and yet so far away.

Dean avoided her the next few days, speaking to her only on business matters. He was seldom in the office, spending his days out with the men on the range. He came in the house often after they were through eating supper and Mrs. Mac fixed him a plate of warmed-over food, which he ate in the den, while the rest of the family watched television or read.

However, by the time the next Sunday rolled around, he seemed more relaxed and once again accompanied them to church. Dorine's heart was heavy as she examined how she could have changed the conversation out there on the range, but in her heart, she knew there was no other way to reach him but by her own personal testimony.

The hot days of June slipped into an even hotter July, with the pace of the office picking up as they filled contracts for the rough stock to go to various rodeos around the mid-west. But nothing could fill the emptiness in her heart except the warm smile of a certain all-around cowboy.

The sound of boots clomping down the stairs before an early July dawn brought Dorine up from a delicious dream to reality—today was the start of the Black Hills Roundup! And they were going! She leaped out of bed, took a quick shower, dressed, made her bed, braided her hair and put personal items into her overnight bag. Her other things were already out in the fifth-wheeler, where she would stay while at the Roundup in Belle Fourche. Dean, Darrell and a couple of the men would bed down in the combination horse trailer with living quarters.

Grabbing her purse, she headed downstairs for the hearty breakfast Mrs. Mac and Marci had put on the table for them. As they rose from the table, Marci held out her arms. "Let's gather 'round for prayer," indicating Dorine should join the family and Mrs. Mac in the circle of prayer. Dorine chanced a glance at Dean, and was surprised to see him with hands folded, head bowed and eyes closed. Was he softening his heart towards the Lord?

After prayer for safety in traveling and God's watchful care while competing, Marci hugged each of them. Dorine's heart was full of emotion at the older woman's kindness, how she always included Dorine as naturally as she did her own children.

"Dorine rides with me," Dean said as he put his dress Stetson on, and gestured for her to precede him.

"Don't I have any say in the matter?" she asked defiantly, picking up her purse. "Maybe I want to ride with Darrell!" How dare he ignore her all this time, then just assume she'd jump when he snapped his fingers!

"Nope, the guys are riding with him," Dean answered smoothly as he held the door open and gave her a sweeping bow, extending his hand for her to go ahead of him. He grinned at the irritated look she threw at him as she stormed passed. He winked at his mother and turned to follow Dorine out. Marci sighed, wondering when Dean would *ever* stop teasing Dorine.

As they drove down the lane in the fresh morning air, Dorine settled her purse on her lap, looking straight ahead. "After days of not talking to me, all of a sudden you decide I exist. What makes you think I want to ride with you? Do you ever consider anyone else's feelings?"

Intent on guiding the heavy-duty pickup through the gate onto the road, he answered absently as he glanced in the side view mirror, "Sure I do, but you're nicer looking than any of the hands...besides, you smell better." He spared her a quick look and smiled, a smile that reached clear up to his eyes. She'd missed that smile and decided to ignore the fact that he'd sidestepped her first question. "I like that lilac scent you wear," he added. With that smile and that charm, how could any woman resist him? She glanced at his dear familiar face and an intense yearning clutched her heart, a yearning to be at his side forever—she knew she'd never feel at home anywhere else than here with him.

Turning her head to gaze blindly out the window, she hoped he wouldn't notice her tremble. Because at that moment, in the cab of a ranch pickup going down a dusty country road, she knew without a doubt that she was in love with this aggravating, manipulating, domineering cowboy! There was no longer any doubt about it—*she was in love!* The air in the cab seemed too warm and too close, she couldn't breath properly. Is this how love happened, like a lightning bolt from heaven?

"Don't be mad at me, prairie chick," Dean wheedled, mistaking her silence for anger. "Let's forget about the ranch today, the business—everything! Let's just have fun this weekend!" He took his eyes off the road to glance at her, a warm sparkle in his eyes. "Remember all those mornings we loaded horses in the dark and drove half the day?" She tried to focus on his deep voice recounting past adventures when they both competed at rodeos all over the west. Intensely aware of his closeness, she was helpless to stop the languid warmth that she was drowning in, tentatively exploring the tenderness of her newly-discovered love.

"Hey! Are you even listening to me?" She jerked to attention. What had she missed? His eyes were on the road but he glanced over at her and winked. "Here I am, pouring out all the rodeo trivia that I can think of, and you're admiring the scenery!" She relaxed slightly. Good. He hadn't guessed her secret. Then a horrible new thought struck her—*how was she going to keep him from finding out?!!*

When she remained silent, Dean wondered what was going through her pretty little head. Her lovely face had an odd expression, one he hadn't ever seen before, so even though he continued talking, he was visualizing that this is the way it would be if they were married—her by his side…only sitting closer. He signaled and turned the pickup onto the freeway ramp, checking the rearview mirror as he sped up. "Do you want to stop at Wall for anything?"

She managed a slight smile. "It's too early in the morning for a free glass of ice water." He laughed and unexpectedly took her hand, sending a jolt clear up to her shoulder! It felt like her whole arm was sizzling! Trying to calm herself, she concentrated on the history of the town of Wall, South Dakota, that had been put on the map over 50 years ago when an enterprising young Ted Hustad had posted signs along the highway, advertising a "glass of free ice water if you stop at Hustad's Drug in Wall, just a few miles ahead!" With her fingers clasped warmly in Dean's hand, Dorine fought to remain calm. *Wouldn't he laugh if he knew she'd lost her heart to him!*

"*Is* something wrong?" He was peering at her with an anxious expression, then swung his gaze back to the road.

"No!" she quickly reassure him. "I-I'm just…"

"I hope you're not going to say 'wool-gathering' again, Dorine! I've told you before that you can't say that to a cattleman!" He grinned at her as he removed his hand so he could guide the pickup around a slow-moving car. "By the way, if you get sleepy, there's a pillow behind the seat." She immediately missed the comfort of that strong hand holding hers, and curled her fingers in frustration. His concern for her well-being and comfort touched her…*but he's always done courteous things for you*, that little voice argued.

To hide her feelings, she reached in the back for the pillow, moved closer to the door and punched the pillow into place. Feigning sleep, she tried to bring her churning emotions under control.

Dean had always been attentive to her—a forgotten memory suddenly sprang to mind—she as an eight-year-old, being lifted off his horse, and before setting her on the ground, his lips brushed her temple. She'd never considered his occasional chaste "pecks" any more than brotherly affection… other memories began to surface…how lingering his hugs were when she, as a teen, did well in barrel-racing competition; a casual arm thrown over her shoulder as they'd watched rodeo events; a hug and kiss on the cheek when she'd been elected cheerleader. However, she had to remember that the DeFoes were an affectionate family, open with their feelings. She shouldn't read too much into what he did.

When he slowed to take the exit at a rest area, she sat up, blinking. The sun had risen behind them, flooding the countryside with golden promises for the day. They got out to stretch their legs, check the horses and share snacks they'd packed. Darrell was full of jokes and wisecracks, and the two men riding with him rolled their eyes. "Help! Rescue us! We've had to listen to this ever since we left Silverdale!"

"Tough!" Dean showed no sympathy. "Better you than us!"

"Hey!" Darrell sputtered at his employees. "You guys wanna ride back there with the horses? Being the boss has its advantages, you know!" The men groaned and held their hands up in defeat.

They climbed back in the vehicles to travel on westward, turning north past Rapid City at the eastern edge of the Black Hills. Dorine couldn't seem to find any topic of conversation, but Dean appeared content with the comfortable silence, or to just hum along with western tunes on the radio.

After leaving the freeway at Spearfish, he guided the caravan through holiday traffic, slowing as they entered Belle Fourche. They took the left turn that put them on the street to the Roundup Grounds, expansive green areas surrounded by towering cottonwoods. It was a stark contrast to the brown landscape through which they'd been traveling all morning.

Once they were parked, horses unloaded and the fifth-wheeler leveled, Dorine left the guys to it—they had plenty of work cut out for them before the big day tomorrow. She needed time away to examine her new feelings. However, some of her former competitors in rodeo events spotted her and she was surrounded by friends who whisked her away to eat, talk and laugh all afternoon.

The sun was lower in the sky when she returned to the fifthwheeler, glancing briefly at the carnival set up downtown across the sun-dappled field from the fairgrounds. Blaze greeted her with tossing head. "Hi, did you miss me?" she reached through the poles to scratch his chin, glad he wouldn't have to put up with biting mosquitoes—the campground area had been sprayed, a blessed relief for all.

"He doesn't seem to mind the new surroundings." Dean ambled around the end of the corral. "It's been awhile since he's been exposed to this," nodding towards sounds coming from the carnival.

His nearness brought an unaccustomed shyness, an emotion foreign to her before she'd realized her love for him. She could only nod and try to take herself in hand.

"Well, hi...there you are," came a throaty voice from behind them and they both turned to see a stunning red-headed woman coming toward them, dressed in slim jeans and a red-striped shirt.

"Hello," smiled Dean, but his heart took a nosedive—*Go away, I want this time with my girl*! Instead, he gallantly introduced the woman. "This is Jackie Watkins, Dorine. She's a producer from one of the stations in Rapid. I met her when I was helping with publicity for the 4-H Fair a few years back." Dorine's heart missed a beat—only a dummy could have missed the admiration in his voice.

Jackie extended her hand and warmly shook hands with Dorine. Her smile reached her friendly green eyes as she said, "I've heard so much about you, I feel that I know you." Her well-modulated voice was sincere, not at all what Dorine would have expected.

*So this is the redhead that Darrell mentioned*. Dorine felt a surge of what she didn't want to identify as jealousy. Schooling her features to politeness, she replied, "I'm happy to meet you. But I'm at a disadvantage—I know nothing about *you*!" she replied, glancing at Dean, who scratched his ear and squinted off into the distance.

She didn't doubt that he was clearly surprised by Jackie's appearance, and if she read him right, not exactly pleased.

The other woman's soft laugh hung in the air. "I've been with the station for *some* time," she replied, as though Dorine should know.

Dean rushed to fill in the awkward silence. "She's got one of the sharpest minds in the industry—do you remember that ad campaign awhile back, with the dog and parrot? That was Jackie's idea." He didn't realize he'd just put his foot in his mouth.

A faint blush spread over the other woman's face. "If a person really likes what they do, it shows." She glanced coyly through long lashes at Dean, and this time, there was no mistaking the jealousy that surged through Dorine! Should she leave? She cleared her throat. "I have to get *our* supper started...would you like to eat with us?" she tossed out the half-hearted invitation.

"Oh, don't go yet—is this your horse?" Jackie gestured towards Blaze. When Dorine nodded, Jackie stepped closer, her eyes moving over the sleek animal. "It has to be yours, because it isn't Dean's." *She'd dropped that little bit of knowledge oh so cleverly.* "Does he mind strangers touching him?"

"No, he's never acted up around anyone," Dorine replied, trying to keep her face expressionless. "Unless he gets spooked."

"Dorine has done an excellent job of training him," Dean said, with a hint of pride and a wink at Dorine. Her stomach plummeted and her heart went into overdrive. However, he'd expressed pride in Jackie's work too—but she already knew how thoughtful he was of others' feelings. However, there *was* something between the two, some kind of connection that she couldn't put her finger on— it appeared that competing in barrel-racing wasn't the only thing she'd missed out on these last few years!

"Do you ride?" she asked the redhead pleasantly.

"Oh, no," Jackie laughed softly as she stroked the horse's head. Blaze turned his nose and sniffed at her, then shook his head. "No, I haven't had time to learn, but I surely do admire them. Dean has taught me what little bit I do know."

This time, even Dean didn't miss the subtle hint that there was more between them than actual fact. "Dorine was riding before she walked. Her father tied her in the saddle with her diaper," he gave Dorine a lazy look. He used his thumb to tip his hat back farther back and the corner of his mouth twitched, an endearing action that tugged at Dorine's heart—*how come she'd never noticed before?!*

Dean hoped he'd redeemed himself after watching the confused expressions play across Dorine's face and realized that Jackie's hints had hit home. He'd taken the redhead out for dinner soon after meeting her, but seeing that she was attracted to him, he'd tried to discourage her without hurting her feelings.

However, he had to hand it to her for her professionalism, even though she didn't stir his blood the way a certain tall brunette did. During the past four lonely years while waiting for Dorine, he would occasionally bump into Jackie at various functions; however, he hoped that his friendly-but-hands-off attitude would alert her to the fact that all she could *ever* expect from him was friendship. He'd never asked her out again, but she seemed to pop up whenever he participated in a rodeo in the vicinity of Rapid City. At times, her presence irritated him as she still seemed to harbor thoughts of romance, and right now was one of those moments. Why else was she sticking around, making sly innuendoes to Dorine?

He smiled at Dorine. "I'll go find Darrell so we can eat." He touched the brim of his hat, hoping Jackie would get the hint.

"I was about to go anyway, I'll walk with you," Jackie said quickly.

Slipping her hand through the crook of Dean's arm, she smiled warmly at Dorine. "It was a pleasure to meet you."

Dorine felt awkward and tongue-tied. "Likewise," she said in her best-manners voice, but the other two had already started to turn away. *Well, I didn't lie, Lord, I am glad to know her...now I'll know who Dean is with when he comes to Rapid. But that doesn't make me feel any better...I really need Your help here, Lord!*

She was grateful that evening for the distraction of an elderly couple, long-time rodeo friends parked next to them, as they all sat around outside eating supper. She wondered if Dean was wishing he'd taken Jackie to a quiet spot by themselves, but he was contentedly settled in a chair next to her—alone. Every time he brushed against her, a million watt jolt zinged along her nerves. She concentrated on the carnival sounds drifting across the grounds, as well as the delicious aromas of cotton candy and tangy barbecue.

"That carnival has been coming to Belle for over 50 years," said the elderly woman from her lawn chair. "When I lived at Vale," she named a small town in the southern part of Butte County, "I used to come with my boyfriends during the week of the Fourth. They loved to get me up there on that Ferris wheel and hope it would stop at the top so they could hug me when I squealed!" Everyone laughed and the conversation moved smoothly along.

Later, instead of strolling over to the carnival with the older couple, Dorine hung back, taking her time to clean up. She didn't want to be a fifth wheel if Dean had arranged to meet Jackie over there. Darrell rushed off to a meeting of the Cowboy Branch of Christian Athletes in Action, but Dean seemed in no hurry as he leisurely helped store the perishables.

When he took a container out of her hands and set it down, she nervously raised her eyes. Putting his hands on her shoulders, he gazed down at her in the subdued light. "Leave the rest of this, we can do it when we come back—let's go over to the carnival. I want to get you up on the Ferris wheel and see if *you* squeal." He grinned mischievously and Dorine's heart flipped over.

"You know I'm not afraid of anything!"

"All too well!" he agreed wryly. "You going to change clothes? You look fine the way you are."

"Stop trying to make decisions for me!" she fumed.

He loved the sparkle in her eyes when she was irritated with him, but he'd rather see a sparkle of desire, letting him know she was aware of him. But for now, he'd settle for just a relaxing evening of no sparring. "Okay." He grinned, satisfied with the confused look she threw his way.

They wandered along the mid-way, his hand in the small of her back to guide her through the rowdy teens that were attempting to impress their girl friends with their prowess at the different carnival booths. She felt enervated every time he brushed against her, and hoped she wouldn't embarrass herself by collapsing at his feet! When he took her hand, it was all she could do not to melt!

He won her a panda bear by knocking all the milk bottles over, and she outdid him in the duck shoot. He relished the triumphant look in her eyes and brushed off the kidding remarks of men who would be his competition tomorrow. "I bow to the competition," he remarked and winked. "But not in the arena," he added with a significant look towards the men. To the sound of their hooting and catcalls, he guided Dorine towards the Ferris wheel.

"Up you go," he whispered in her ear as they got into their seat and the roustabout clamped the bar across them. "Are you going to scream and clutch wildly at me?" He waggled his eyebrows.

She slanted him a meaningful glance. "In your dreams, cowboy!" But she couldn't help a small giggle that escaped her lips. She was *very* conscious of his arm across her back as the wheel lifted them up into the night sky. The music and sounds of the carnival seemed far below them, the glitter and glamour fading as a soft breeze caressed her cheeks. She'd worn her hair down and it drifted in shiny waves over the shoulders of her sleeveless western-style blouse. A few strands blew gently across his face and he raised a hand to brush them away, his knuckles grazing her cheek. A bright flush swept over her face and she hoped that he hadn't seen it in the shadows. Intensely aware of his silent gaze, she searched frantically for something to say to burst the bubble of the romantic night.

"I suppose you're waiting for me to screech and clutch at you?" she dared a look at him.

"That would be nice," he surprised her by saying. His eyes held a warm tenderness that made her nervous. What was he up to now?

The Ferris wheel suddenly jerked to a stop and her move towards him was involuntary. He immediately put his arms around her and drew her closer. "I won't let anything happen to you, prairie chick," he whispered, his lips brushing her ear. For the life of her, she couldn't speak or move. "I've always been here for you, you know that, don't you?" His words were husky and full of emotion. The warm night wove a spell around them, a spell that was drawing her deeper and deeper into the bubble of romance.

"Yes, you have." She turned and looked up at him. Their faces were close, their lips only inches apart. She couldn't seem to breathe or tear her gaze away from him—

The Ferris wheel jerked again, shattering the spell and setting their chair to swinging.

"Whoa! What's going on down there?!" Dean exclaimed as he leaned forward to peer over the edge. She moved slightly away from him just as the wheel jerked again, then began a smooth glide down to the ground. Dorine swallowed hard and tried to calm her skittering emotions. She clutched the bar in front of her as Dean adjusted his hat and leaned back, his arms crossed over his chest. "Not scared, huh?" His blue gaze twinkled at her.

She tossed her head. "It surprised me, is all," she tried for aloofness. His chuckle told her he didn't believe her. She was glad when they were at last able to step off the wheel and she turned to him. "I'm ready to call it a night but you can stay if you want."

He shook his head. "No, I'll walk you back."

"You don't have to—"

He gripped her arm and began walking. "Dorine, you know how crazy some of these guys get with a few beers under their belt. I'll see that you get safely back."

Secretly, she was pleased at his gallant gesture. She was never dependent on anyone for anything, but it felt kind of nice to be cared for and to have this feeling of being cherished.

They walked silently to the edge of the crowd and crossed the dusty street lined with vehicles of carnival-goers. Once on the other side, the semi-darkness closed about them as they made their way to the well-lit campgrounds. "Did you have fun tonight?" he asked as they came to the fifth-wheeler.

She put her key in the lock and turned to him. "Yes, I did. Thanks." Was that *her* voice sounding so breathless?

"I did too." Dorine went weak from the warmth in his eyes and had to remind her heart to beat. "We don't take time to play very often," he added. "I'm glad you could let your hair down tonight," and she held her breath as his gaze moved over her hair. "I like it that way...makes a—" he stopped abruptly, his eyes coming back to hers.

Why, all of a sudden, couldn't she come up with some witty retort?!! His face filled her vision, those beloved eyes, so tender.

He slowly bent toward her and gently kissed the tip of her nose. The brief contact sent shock waves through her before he stepped back. He smiled, tapped her nose with his finger and said, "Sleep well, little one." Then he walked away.

She watched him go, still speechless, before she finally turned and went up the last step.

Around back of the trailer, he waited and smiied when he heard the door click shut. He hoped he'd put her off balance, and from her lack of response, indignant or otherwise, he'd maybe just succeeded.

# CHAPTER TWELVE

Dorine was up early the morning of the Fourth. No wonder, she'd taken forever to fall asleep, confusion romping through her—why *hadn't* he kissed her? He must have seen she was more than willing! While she brushed Blaze's coat until it shone, she could see nothing but Dean's face last night. They'd always been friends, but now she wanted more—could *he* ever give more? She winced—he knew all the good and the bad about her—*especially* the bad—her temper, her stubbornness, *everything*—could he feel anything for her after all that? Mulling through her dark thoughts, she put the decorative bridle on Blaze, and quickly saddled him.

The guys had grabbed a quick breakfast over at the chuckwagon but she was too nervous to eat much more than a little fruit before getting dressed to ride in the parade. Since she was among the group of former rodeo queens to be honored, she slipped the sparkly white "Miss Jackson County Rodeo Queen" banner over her green satin shirt and eyed herself in the mirror. She'd chosen to wear her hair loose and flowing almost to her waist, hoping it wouldn't be too hot over her shoulders. Hearing Dean's familiar whistle, she took a calming breath and grabbed her white Stetson.

He was waiting for her, holding the reins of their saddled horses, and his breath caught when he saw her in the early morning sun. "You're beautiful, prairie chick," his voice sounded husky and low, filled with wonder.

She tried to ignore the way her heart plummeted towards her stomach, and greedily drank in the sight of him in a white western shirt, black pants and white hat. Every time she saw him, she fell deeper in love. Aware of her outright ogling him, she jerked her eyes away before taking the reins and mounting Blaze with lithe gracefulness. "You're not too shabby yourself," she quipped. He mounted Black and sat gazing at her. "What, is something wrong?" She touched her hat and frowned.

He reached over to run his hand over her hair and across her shoulder. "You don't often wear your hair loose and I haven't told you lately how beautiful it is. I'm glad you've never cut it." The moment was frozen in time as they looked at each other. Darrell's rude whistle brought them back to their surroundings. Dorine ground her teeth—he had the most *obnoxious* way of showing up at the wrong times!

"Hey, you guys gonna take all day? Let's get moving!" He pranced Jinx up next to Dorine and gave a low drawn-out wolf whistle. "You clean up pretty good, cowgirl!"

She glared at him. "So do you, but did you remember to wash behind your ears, you old sheepherder?" He guffawed and readjusted his hat before trotting Jinx off toward the parade route.

Dean grinned after his brother, enjoying the byplay. "Shall we?" he gestured for Dorine to lead the way.

A slight breeze felt welcome, as the mid-morning sun was pouring heat into the pavement. They wove through the parade units and when an errant breeze brought a hint of Dean's cologne, she reminded herself to focus, focus, focus. The clip-clop of the horses' hooves on the pavement helped to steady her concentration.

There was a party atmosphere up and down the parade route, with people calling to each other, running back and forth across the street. Colorful flags swirled in and out, the breeze playfully plucking at the silky folds. Blaze snorted and tossed his head, dancing sideways and crowding Black, who began dancing too. Dean's firm hand on the reins brought the big horse under control, and when the parade marshal gave the signal, the high school band began playing as they marched smartly along, moving the parade towards Main Street.

Dean rode easily, one hand resting on his thigh, nodding to spectators. Dorine's heart swelled with pride as she watched him, so relaxed and completely in his element. When they came abreast of the announcer's booth, introductions blared out of loudspeakers as the stock contractor was acknowledged, the rodeo announcer and other dignitaries. The Black Hills Rodeo Queen gracefully waved her gloved hand when her trick horse gently reared. As it circled, she sent a flirtatious glance Dean's way, but Dorine was pleased to see that he never noticed. In fact, he didn't even seem aware of the unit ahead of them: the very beautiful Miss Rodeo South Dakota and Miss Rodeo America.

"Now, we have several world champions," blared the loudspeaker. "The World High School and also College Champion barrel racer from a few years ago, Dorine Andrews of the Circle A Ranch down at Sil-ver-dale, South Dakota," the announcer drew out his words. "She was also Miss Jackson County Rodeo Queen before going off to college. Hi, Dorine!" She waved at the officials in the high booth, then gave a wave to the crowds. Blaze seemed to know that he was center stage, prancing and proudly arching his neck.

"Riding with her is Dean DeFoe, also from Silverdale," went on the announcer's voice, "World Champion All-Around Cowboy for three consecutive years! World Champion in all the rodeo events while in high school, and he holds almost all the World Champion College Rodeo titles." Dean waved at the crowd, who whistled and applauded in appreciation while Black strained at the reins, tossing his head.

The parade moved quickly along and they turned into a quiet side street to return to the Roundup grounds at a brisk trot.

A buffet lunch was served back of the grandstand, with people milling about as they carried full plates of food to shady spots. Many of the contestants seemed to inhale their food without appreciation, others never ate at all, their focus on the afternoon of competition ahead of them. Sun glistened off sequins and spangles on colorful shirts, and competitor's numbers fluttered on their backs or pants as the cowboys began moving towards the arena.

Dean had followed Dorine through the buffet line and they'd eaten with a group of friends from Big Horn County in Montana, leaving no time for private conversation. Just as well, she thought, her brain had run out of intelligent things to push out her mouth!

Since they were both riding in the opening ceremonies, they'd left their horses saddled and watered while they ate. Dean checked Blaze's cinch before mounting Black, and turned to catch Dorine's glare. Putting his hands up in surrender, he chuckled. "Just checking, just checking!"

She grabbed the reins and put her foot into the stirrup, trying to push down her irritation. She was finding it hard to rid herself of old habits and had to sternly take herself in hand. He was only being solicitous, she reminded herself.

Those in the grand entry were milling around behind the grandstand, their horses' hooves churning dust where the sprinkler truck has missed wetting the ground. Dorine rode into the arena beside Dean and looked out over the stands full of people. It was like a patchwork quilt, with different colors sprinkled through the seats. A breeze swirled the South Dakota state flag she carried, and when her name was announced, she carried it at a fast gallop around the inside perimeter of the fence to the applause and cheers of the crowd. Then she was out of the arena and done with official duties. Dean would ride Black in competition so he waved jauntily to her before trotting around behind the chutes. She took Blaze to the corral near the fifth-wheeler, unsaddled him and gave him water before hurrying back to the stands.

Dean was looking for her when she arrived, and came to stand beside her when the events started, casually draping his arm around her shoulders, just as he'd done countless times. He appeared to have no idea of his effect on her—it was a good thing *she* wasn't competing, her bones had turned to jelly!

The brothers were entered in several events, with good-natured joshing between them. They both placed well, Darrell winning one event and Dean another, then they tied for a third.

Lastly, came the event that everyone waited for—bull riding. Dorine had seen many men, including her dad, ride the wild-looking animals, but this was the first time her heart was so involved.

When Dean's bull burst out of the chute, bucking and fishtailing, she whispered "Hang on, honey, hang on." She had climbed to the end of the bleachers and was tightly gripping the edge of her seat as her eyes followed the action in the arena. The bull snorted, whipping this way and that, trying to dislodge the hated rider from his back. The whistle sounded but the danger wasn't over—Dean still had to get off and away from the raging bull. His hat went sailing before the bull took one last jump, and off he went into the dirt. The bull turned, his eyes filled with rage, his horns down. The crowd gasped and Dorine held her fingers over her mouth, her heart in her throat.

Saviors of many a bull rider, the rodeo clowns came running and jumped between the bull and Dean as he scrambled out of the way. The furious animal turned its head and chased one of the clowns, who hopped into a nearby escape barrel. The crowd roared its approval and applauded as Dean clamored up on the fence like everyone else in the path of the bull.

Dorine realized she'd scarcely breathed during the eight-second ride, every muscle in her body tensed, as though *she* had been on the bull. She dropped her hand, willing herself to relax. Dean had been hurt before in competition, nothing serious, she reminded herself. And the ride was over, for heaven's sake! Relax!

After a couple of more riders, it was Darrell's turn. Dean was up on the chute, helping get the agitated bull calmed as it snorted and tried to dislodge Darrell even before the chute gate was opened. It took several more minutes until the bull settled down, then suddenly the chute gate swung open and the ride began.

The bull bucked as it turned out the gate, and ran into the arena a few yards, leaped to turn in mid-air and whipped it's body. Round and round, back and forth, until Dorine thought poor Darrell would snap in two. The whistle sounded and Darrell dove off.

But the bull was so enraged nothing would stop it, and it turned, head down, moving like a locomotive towards the fallen man. This time, the clowns were just a split second late, and the wicked-looking horns plowed into Darrell's side. Dorine was on her feet, screaming along with the rest of the crowd. *Dear Lord, no!* The clowns danced in front of the bull, waving their arms and shouting. It stopped and swung its massive head from one clown to the other. Darrell lay in a fetal position, not moving, at the feet of the bull. *Heavenly Father, protect him!* She prayed. Suddenly, the animal took off after one of the clowns, but Dorine's eyes never left Darrell. *Why didn't he get up?* The crowd grew silent and a hush settled along with the dust drifting over the arena floor.

Dean was over the fence and running while he eyed the bull, which thankfully, was heading towards an open gate.

He dropped to his knees beside Darrell. "Hey, man, you okay?" Other cowboys gathered beside him as he gravely examined the broken skin and blood visible through the rip in Darrell's shirt.

Darrell rolled over, straightening one leg and grimacing. "My side... feels like it's on fire," he gulped out. Dean stood and waved at the stock contractor, who waved back even as he barked orders.

Dorine's fists were clenched tightly together over her mouth as she watched a group of men run into the arena with a stretcher. They worked over Darrell for what seemed an agonizingly long time before they carefully lifted him to a backboard. Four men slowly carried him to the gate that Dean had gone ahead to open. Dorine continued to pray as she scrambled off the bleachers, hardly aware of the crowd around her on its feet with ear-splitting applause. Squeezing between people to get to the ambulance, she saw Dean scanning the crowd and knew when he spotted her.

"Is he hurt bad?" her voice was strangled and laced with fear as she clutched at his shirtfront.

"He's okay," he soothed, holding her close, his head lowered next to her ear. "Probably some cracked ribs, and he's bleeding a little, so he'll need stitches...but he'll be all right."

"Are you just trying to make me feel better?" she switched her gaze from the ambulance to look up with fearful eyes.

He smiled. "No, because he wanted to know if he'd beaten my time."

The air whooshed out of her lungs and she sagged in relief.

"Hey!" Dean caught her with one arm around her waist. "I said he'd be all right!" He put both arms around her, savoring the closeness. "They're taking him to the emergency room...he'll be *all right*, Dorine!"

"I want to go to the hospital with him," she croaked weakly, not even noticing the interested glances of bystanders.

"Okay, I'll tell them you're going in the ambulance with him. I'll bring the pickup." He reluctantly released her, spoke to the attendants and helped her into the ambulance. He switched from worry about Darrell to thinking about having to call his mother, even knowing she would take it in stride. After all, she'd been a rancher/rodeo wife herself.

In the ambulance, Dorine leaned over Darrell. "You big macho sheepherder, now look what you've done!" she scolded softly.

His eyes resembled deep blue pools in his white face. "Didn't move fast enough, cowgirl," he tried to joke feebly. When he saw her stricken face, he pulled an arm out from under the blanket and gripped her hand. "Hey, I'm all right, don't take it so hard!"

Later, she paced in the waiting room near the emergency room cubicles while Darrell had x-rays. Nurses walked by on soft-soled shoes, the elevator beeped as it came and went amongst the distant hum of machines. Darrell didn't have a life-and-death situation but the worry never lessened, just the same.

The outside doors swung open, and expecting to see Dean, she was startled to see Sharry Schafer walking swiftly towards her.

"Where is he?" the petite blonde demanded, her blue eyes worried.

Dorine pointed. "He's in x-ray, so I don't know anything yet."

Sharry made a visible effort to pull herself together and breathed out slowly. "I was so scared when I saw that bull going after him."

"*You* were at the rodeo?" exclaimed Dorine as she led the way to the vinyl-covered seats along one wall.

"Yes," Sharry replied shakily. "I couldn't stay away, not when I knew he intended to ride a bull today." She sank down gratefully.

"He...told you that?" Dorine asked hesitantly, settling beside her.

"Yes...he...ah...came to see me last weekend," Sharry's voice came out in a whisper. "I wish now...I hadn't argued with him," she said glumly, watching the double doors to the emergency room.

"His injuries didn't look all that bad," Dorine tried to soothe her. "I wouldn't worry. He was conscious the whole time coming here."

Sharry shrugged, then turned to look across the hall to the nurses' station. "I don't know why he always has to be such a daredevil, he doesn't take *anything* seriously—and he's *always* wanting me to come back home! Why can't he understand my calling is here?!! I…" She stopped suddenly, her eyes narrowing as Dean walked in, his face registering surprise when he saw her sitting with Dorine.

His gaze flicked to the double doors leading to the emergency room. "He's still in there?" When Dorine nodded, he walked over and sat beside her, taking off his hat and brushing a hand over his disheveled hair.

"Do you want me to call your mother?" Dorine spoke softly.

"Already did, she's okay," he sighed, leaning back, giving Sharry a sideways glance. "I told her Darrell's getting slow in his old age and the bull was younger."

Sharry pursed her lips and looked away. Dean shot a questioning glance at Dorine, who took his hand and squeezed it, giving a slight shake of her head. Dean turned his palm up, wrapping his fingers around hers and returning the squeeze. A warmth swept up her arm at his touch but it wouldn't occur to her until later that it seemed as natural as breathing to reach for Dean's hand—they didn't need words to communicate.

After a few minutes of silence, he asked if he could get either of them coffee and they both nodded. When he was gone, Sharry cleared her throat. "You two seem to be pretty cozy." She glanced meaningfully at Dorine's hand.

Feeling herself blush, Dorine shrugged. "Our families have always done things together, especially rodeos, ever since I can remember." Sharry made a scoffing sound, turning her eyes back towards the emergency room doors again. Dorine took a deep breath. "Sharry, you don't have to be mad at Dean, he's not Darrell."

"He's the one that's influenced him, though!" Her sharp reply was out of character, but seeing Dorine's puzzled look, she relented. "Darrell thinks he has to live up to his big brother's image!"

"Did *he* tell you that?"

Sharry squirmed in her seat and looked down. "No-o-o…"

"How do you figure, then?"

Sharry turned angry eyes towards Dorine. "Why else would he risk his life at doing dumb things like riding bulls, and bucking horses, and…who knows what else?!!"

Dorine gave a half-laugh. "But Sharry, that's what ranching is all about. It's part of their life, what they do on a ranch every day—just like you love nursing and it's what you do, this is their life too."

"That's different!" Sharry insisted, fiddling with her purse strap.

"Why is it different?" Dorine persisted.

"Because. There's no danger in what I do," her voice trailed off.

"Let me play the devil's advocate here," Dorine said, shifting in her chair. "What about when they bring in someone who's bloody from a fight? Isn't there a danger of you getting AIDS or some other disease from that blood? What about when a drug addict goes wild and fights to get up off the stretcher, hitting you in the process? What about—"

Sharry held up her hand. "All right all ready, you've made your point. But I don't deliberately get on a wild bull then let it gore me when I fall off."

"He didn't fall, he jumped," Dorine said quietly, an imp of mischief getting hold of her tongue.

"Whatever, same thing," Sharry replied, shrugging uncaringly.

Only a dummy couldn't see she *did* care. "Here's our coffee."

Dean handed them the cups, then sat as they sipped the hot brew in silence. In a few minutes, a doctor came out of the double doors, and all three rose to their feet. He announced that even though Darrell had two broken ribs, he was fine—but, he wanted to keep him in the hospital overnight to watch for infection.

Sharry listened with a stoic face, then turned to Dorine. "Thanks for the coffee." She put her cup down and turned to leave.

"Aren't you even going to stay and see him?" Dorine asked.

Sharry walked away, lifting her hand and waving her fingers back over her shoulder as the doctor shook hands with Dean and nodded at Dorine before leaving.

Dean looked at the door through which Sharry had disappeared and turned back to Dorine, raising his eyebrows in question.

"You know what the problem is between those two?" she said triumphantly, tossing her hair over her shoulder.

"And it is?" Dean raised his cup and looked at her over the rim.

"Stubbornness."

Dean choked, coffee slopping over the side of his cup. "Stubbornness?" he repeated, wiping his shirtfront.

"Yep! Good old-fashioned stubbornness!"

"It takes one to know one," he murmured, stepping back.

She ignored his words *and* his retreat. "She's thrown up this smokescreen about not wanting to date him because she's afraid he's going to get hurt and she loves him too much to stand by and watch that happen." Dorine's eyes softened with a faraway look.

"Do *you* ever worry about him…or me?" He unashamedly fished.

"I haven't…really…before today," she admitted quietly. "Those bulls are so unpredictable…" she shook her head.

A nurse glided towards them and said they could go in to see Darrell, but Dean wished she had delayed her message just a few more minutes. Since arriving at the Roundup, the atmosphere between he and Dorine had subtly changed, and he was impatient to talk with her, explore these new feelings. But he needed more time and privacy than what was afforded here.

In his room, Darrell was still feeling woozy from the anesthesia.

"Did you get the license number of that truck?" he asked weakly.

"Now I know you're going to be all right," Dorine laughed softly.

He lifted his other hand and wiped it over his face. "Hoooie, do I ever smart!" He looked up at the IV. "Does *that* mean they think I'm staying here? *No way*, I'm going home now…*today!*"

Dean put a hand on his shoulder. "The doctor said the gash on your side was kind of deep and they need to keep you under observation."

Darrell groaned and glanced away. "I've been hurt worse than this and didn't have to stay in the hospital." His eyelids drooped.

Dean chuckled, knowing he'd have to stay awhile and convince his brother to stay in the bed. Glancing at Dorine, he saw the fatigue in her eyes and realized that the day's traumatic events had taken their toll on her—she needed to go lay down.

He fished his keys out of his pocket. "Here, take the pickup back to the rodeo grounds, I'll walk over." He paused, looking down at her, his gaze roaming over her face and coming to rest on her lips. Frustration welled up in him as he realized he'd have to postpone once again, the words that were in his heart. A hospital room was no place to carry on the conversation that he wanted to have with her.

Dorine was holding her breath as she gazed into his eyes, waiting, waiting...for what? A regretful expression crossed his face and he stepped back. "You better take the horses home today, I think we're done rodeoing for this Fourth. I'll stay in the fifth-wheeler tonight. The guys can have a couple of days off and stay too, unless you want them to go along in case you have trouble?"

She blinked. *He was dismissing her*! Irritation erupted—who did he think he was, ordering her to leave? Maybe she wanted to stay *too*!! She glanced at Darrell's dozing form and swallowed the heated words waiting to bubble out. "I've never needed help before, why would I need it now?!" she snapped, keeping her voice low. As she turned away, she knew that part of her irritation was wanting him to say what was on his mind—*why didn't he just spit it out?!!*

Taken by surprise with her sudden change of mood, Dean wondered what he'd said or done to cause the shift. "Dorine?"

"Never mind!" she replied and swept out the door, letting it swoosh closed behind her. He rubbed his hand over his neck and sighed.

Once back at the campground, she straightened the inside of the fifthwheeler, checked on foodstuffs, then put her things into her duffle bag. Their men had taken all the horses back to the campground after the rodeo, and by the time she was ready, she heard Dean bringing the ranch pickup and trailer next to the corrals. She hurried out to carry tack to the trailer while Dean lead first Black, then Blaze, into the trailer. Deftly fastening the rear door, he turned to her. "I left the cell phone lay on the seat," he nodded toward the front of the truck as he took her by the elbow to guide her. "I need to be at the hospital when the doctor makes his rounds tonight."

Opening the driver's door, he helped her up. "You going to be okay?" He finally noticed her silence. She nodded, smiling coolly. He stood looking at her, hands resting on his hips, his eyes searching her face. "Dorine—"

She waited breathlessly. "Yes?" *How quickly hope sprang up!*

"I..." Indecision warred with something else as he gazed at her. Then his hands fell to his sides. "We need to talk after I get home."

Disappointed, she glanced away and swallowed. "Drive careful!" he commanded, slapping the side of the door with his hand.

She eased the pickup into gear and muttered, "No, I'm going to race like I'm at the Indy 500!" He cocked his head in question, but she was already moving away from him on the graveled track.

As she drove out of Belle Fourche toward the freeway, she wondered how a person could feel so much love for someone and still be so *irritated* by them!!

Dean stood watching her leave, wondering if he'd let a golden opportunity slip through his fingers. He didn't think he'd misread the expression in her eyes—she felt something for him too... Shaking his head, he readjusted his hat and determined to keep her out of his mind while he saw to his brother's needs.

# CHAPTER THIRTEEN

Dorine turned the horses over to the ranch hands when she got home later that night, and went immediately into the house to report to Marci and Mrs. Mac. After she'd showered, dressed and had something to eat, she realized that in spite of her irritation, she could hardly wait until Dean's return— *"We need to talk"* rang promisingly in her mind.

But it was not to be—when he returned home the next day with Darrell, he was deluged with business and had to rush off to Texas to take care of an emergency at the ranch there.

The next few days dragged by. Office work, which Dorine normally found challenging, had lost its appeal. The only bright spot was when Melody stopped by with her baby.

Dorine's heart tightened with love when she held the tiny infant, mesmerized by her beautiful blue eyes and creamy soft complexion. The yearning for a family of her own enveloped her and she felt her eyes misting. The urge to have and hold her own baby grew stronger, and as she gazed down at Kimberly, she envisioned her child...with brilliant blue eyes and curly black hair...

"You need to have a baby of your own," Melody whispered as she leaned over to lift Kimberly into her arms. She winked slyly.

Dorine shrugged and smiled. "Some day, some day. Husband first, baby second." When she left, Dorine was filled with an unfamiliar yearning...for family...home...babies...and a certain tall cowboy.

Mid-July was branding time on all the surrounding ranches. It was understood that she would be out of the DD office until branding was done at her ranch, the Circle A. She picked up the vaccine at Vayle's Farm and Feed in town, bought provisions for chuck wagon meals for the hired men, and got her record books out.

The following week was filled with long days in the saddle during roundup and Dorine kept a sharp eye out for signs of anything wrong while out on the range. Were the rustlers still in the area? No one even mentioned it any more and maybe the danger was past. She'd have to ask Bryce why she couldn't move home—her musings were interrupted by an ornery cow breaking away from the herd, and Blaze wheeled to head her off.

There were several days of hard work in the dusty corral as they separated calves from the cows, vaccinated them, castrated the males, dehorned and tagged all of the calves. The air was filled with familiar sounds and scents—men shouting, animals bawling and dust drifting everywhere from under hundreds of churning hooves. Dust settled on her face and arms, and perspiration ran down her back, soaking her shirt as she deftly gave shots to each calf while the men manned the squeeze chute. Once a routine had been established, she did her job automatically while she wondered where Dean was and if he was thinking of her...*We have to talk* echoed in her mind.

Someone tallied the numbers of cows and calves and when they'd finished, she saw that Alfred's estimation of the calf crop was correct—the number was much less than last year. Was this the work of rustlers? Especially since a number of cows were also missing? Her heart sank and fear threatened before she remembered the One who owns the cattle on a thousand hills. He knew that she needed enough animals to take to fall market if she was to keep the ranch operating in the black. *I know You don't need my meddling, Lord, but I can't help wondering how You're going to get me out of this situation. Maybe You don't want me to continue ranching?* Her heart thudded as she thought of that very real possibility. What, then, *was* her future?

The men had turned the bawling calves loose to find their frantic mothers milling outside the corrals, and began herding them back towards the open range. Alfred pulled his hat low and approached her. "Glad that's done for another year," he drawled.

Tucking her fear away, she said, "It's harder on the mama cows than on us. Well, I'm off for a shower as soon as I put the records in the office. Is there anything else we need to do?"

He shook his head. "Nope, nothin' I kin think of." He touched the brim of his hat and turned away. "See ya later."

He sure seemed in a hurry to get away...but he was as itchy hot and dirty as she and probably wanted to get into the shower.

When she got back to the Double D, she walked into a quiet house to take a cold drink from the refrigerator. Marci and Mrs. Mac had gone to visit Maple's sister in Rapid City, but the silence was comforting and she was glad to be back home. She stopped with the glass halfway to her lips. When had she begun to think of this as "home?" Gazing around the familiar kitchen, she remembered learning board games at the big family table... Darcy giving her a home permanent...learning to bake bread under Mrs. Mac's patient tutelage. This is what made a home, not a building, it was...family...and love. Dean's face formed in her mind, that stray curl over his forehead and a wicked gleam in those blue eyes...

As though her thoughts had conjured him up, her ear caught the distant noise of an approaching plane— *he was home!* Her heart thumped and she put her hand on her chest. Would they *finally* get a chance to talk?

The phone rang and when she answered, Robin's distraught voice came over the line. "Dorine? Is Mrs. Mac back from Rapid City?"

"I just walked in the house and there's no one here—what's wrong?" she'd caught the panicky tone of her friend's voice.

"Little Kimberly is running a high fever and Melody called me, but we can't get her temperature down, even with tepid baths. Mrs. Mac always seems to know what to do..."

Dorine's heart plunged with uneasiness. Robin didn't get upset easily. "Has Melody called the doctor at Phillip?"

"She did and they told us to keep on with the baths but to keep them informed... I'm really scared," Robin's voice dropped to a whisper. "She's so tiny, and her pulse is 'way too fast..."

"I don't know what to tell you, Robin," Dorine felt tearful herself. "Let's pray." She closed her eyes and over the phone, the two friends lifted the baby up to the Father in heaven. "I'm going to grab a quick shower but I'll be right here, so call if anything changes!"

Her heart was still beating rapidly as she took the stairs two at a time and rushed through her shower, praying for the tiny infant. Sliding into denim shorts and a white cotton blouse, she was drying her hair when she heard Dean's footsteps in the kitchen below.

She shut off the dryer and ran lightly down the stairs, sweeping her hair up into a ponytail as she went. His eyes lit up when he saw her but his eagerness changed to concern when he saw her fear-filled expression. "What's wrong?"

"Melody's baby is sick, she's running a high fever." She went on to explain the situation as he stared intently at her.

"We need a clinic here, and I hope we get one before something happens to one of us!" Frustration laced his words. "Well," he rubbed the back of his neck, "I'm gonna get a shower. Let me know if something happens." He turned and trudged up the stairs. Her eyes followed him, knowing he was tired…their talk would have to wait…again.

Since Marci and Mrs. Mac weren't back yet, she started supper. Her lips moved in silent prayer as she peeled potatoes and sliced them with onions into a large black frying pan. Getting the meat out of the refrigerator that Mrs. Mac had set to thaw that morning, she shaped hamburger patties and slid them under the broiler. *Melody was so happy just a few days ago, and Kimberly's eyes are such a pretty blue.* She chopped broccoli and cauliflower together, drizzled a honey-mustard dressing over them and adding chopped peanuts.

*Heavenly Father, please hear our prayers for this little one…only You have the power of life or death. Bring down her fever…we thank you, and praise the name of Jesus.*

Dean came downstairs just as Mrs. Mac and Marci drove in the yard. The phone rang and Dorine grabbed it. "Yes?" Her eyes turned fearfully to Dean's as he moved close to her, listening after she turned the phone so they could both hear. Darrell came in, hung his hat up and hesitated, sensing the tension. Dean put his arm across Dorine's shoulders and she handed him the phone, whispering to Darrell, "Melody's baby is really sick…"

Turning her face into Dean's shirt, she drew strength from his solid body and tried to get a grip on her emotions but a soft sob escaped. Dean's arm tightened around her, holding her close to his warmth and comfort. She breathed deeply of the smells that she associated only with him—soap and pine scent—added to that was the steady strong heartbeat that made her want to cuddle up and stay there forever. He could handle anything, he would keep the world at bay. She closed her eyes and curled her fingers against his shirt front.

He shifted her to the side. "Listen Robin....just listen!" he spoke sternly. "Get them into the car and come out here. I'm going to fly her into Rapid. We'll call the doctor and have them waiting at the airport with an ambulance....what?...Bring the boys over here, we'll take care of them—Melody needs you now." He hung up the phone and turned to Darrell. "Can you help me refuel the plane?" A man of quick decisions, Dean had taken over as he always did, mapping out a plan of action. Dorine suddenly realized how everyone within his sphere of influence automatically looked to him—his natural leadership kicked into gear when trouble presented itself.

Darrell nodded and headed for the door, holding it open for his mother and Mrs. Mac. "Melody's baby is real sick ...Dorine'll tell you about it." Marci came in ahead of Mrs. Mac, laden with packages, their faces reflecting concern.

Dean turned, putting both arms around Dorine as though it was the most natural thing in the world to do. Trouble was, she suddenly realized it *was* the most natural thing in the world. But when he began rubbing small circles on her back, her mind went blank—her heart hammered so loud he must surely hear it! She mentally shook herself and tuned in to hear him explain, "Robin said Melody was clutching her like a lifeline and wants her to go along. Paul is working out of the area, they're trying to reach him. Robin can leave the boys here with Dorine," he pulled back and glanced down at her, "I didn't think you'd mind—"

Her mouth felt as dry as Badlands dust but she managed to breathe out, "You know I don't—this is my best friend!" She gazed up into those beautiful intensely blue eyes that were filled with tenderness.

"I knew I could count on you, sweetheart," Dean gave her a

squeeze along with a grateful smile. "Call Dr. Brown and have him make the arrangements for the ambulance." He turned to follow Darrell out the door. She knew that his mind was already on what he had to do... but did he realize he'd called her *sweetheart*?

Her breath caught as the implication sank in and she glanced quickly at Marci to see if she'd caught it. But the older woman's forehead was creased with a frown as she murmured, "We can help most by praying." They bustled to put packages away, then joined hands with Dorine by the kitchen sink to pray.

Afterwards, she rushed up the stairs to slip into her tennis shoes and hurried over to the airstrip.

Darrell had just finished refueling the plane while Dean did a flight check. He saw her running towards them and came to meet her, his eyebrows raised in question. She panted, "No more calls so I guess they're on their way." When he took her by the shoulders, drawing her into a warm embrace, her emotions bubbled over and tears sprang to her eyes.

"Don't worry, sweetheart, we'll take care of that baby," he murmured when he felt her trembling. He stroked her hair and kissed the top of her head, wondering if she'd realized what he called her—suddenly, it didn't matter any more—he was tired of holding back, tired of weighing his words around her. It was time to come clean. "You *are* my sweetheart, aren't you?"

Her heart stopped, then beat in triple time. She raised her head and searched his eyes. There, she saw love—*was it possible he loved her like she loved him? Yes! It was there in his eyes!* She could do nothing more than be as honest as he was. "Yes, I'm your sweetheart," she whispered, her heart soaring into the heavens.

He gazed at her lips and her heart hammered as his head came down and he brushed his mouth over hers in a tantalizing motion that left her wanting more. She raised on her tiptoes, her hand behind his neck to pull him forward and he groaned as he deepened the kiss. Everything around them faded, there was only the two of them. Reluctantly, Dean pulled back and the world gradually came back into focus as Robin's noisy old pickup rattled down the dirt track beside the runway.

"Here they come," he spoke softly while holding her until she regained her balance—one more example of his thoughtfulness.

As Robin screeched to a halt beside them, he stepped back, squeezing her shoulders. "Pray, will you?" The shock of hearing his request reverberated through her—*pray? Dean?*

But he'd already reverted to the man in charge as he turned to help Melody with the baby. Darrell lifted Jason and Jeremy out of the pickup, herding them to the side of the tarmac. Dorine watched them, still in shock—first Dean kissed her socks off, then stunned her with his request for *prayer?!!*

After helping the women into the plane, Dean trotted back to her. He crouched down beside the boys and smiled reassuringly. "Everything will be all right—remember how Mommy taught you to pray?" At their sober nods, he hugged them. "Well, now is the time to do that praying—pray that old Dean can *swoop* through the sky like Santa Claus!" They smiled a little hesitantly, then he stood and gave Dorine a long look. "You and I are *definitely* going to talk when I get back," he promised softly before running back to the plane.

An overpowering love for him flooded through her, and it was all she could do not to blurt out her words of love. Aware of Darrell beside her, she turned to see him grinning at her, his eyes dancing with mischief. "Talk, huh? That didn't look like 'talk' to me!" When she didn't answer, he whooped. "Don't tell me for the first time in your life you're speechless?!!" His teasing brought her back down to earth and she almost elbowed him in the ribs before she realized they were still tender from the gouging the bull had given him.

The plane's engine whined and the wheels began turning. Dean pushed the throttle forward and they moved down the runway, slowly at first, then picking up speed and finally soaring into the soft evening sky, circling toward the west. The little group on the ground watched until it was almost out of sight, then Dorine kneeled to put her arms around the two little boys, who were watching in wide-eyed wonder. Jeremy's lips began to pucker and he raised an arm to point at the speck that was the disappearing plane. "Mommy!" Tears spilled out of his eyes and he began to cry softly.

Darrell squatted down beside him. "Hey, one of these days Dean will take you for a ride, just like he's taking Mommy; would you like that?" Jeremy turned a tear-streaked face to him but stopped crying as he listened to Darrell's soothing voice. Dorine was trembling as she held the toddlers, listening to Darrell's attempts to divert the little boy's attention away from his mother leaving.

"Besides, I've got a new colt to show you. Have you seen any baby horses lately?" Jeremy put his finger in his mouth as he stared at Darrell's mouth. Darrell closed his lips, then snaked his tongue out one side and quickly back in. Jeremy's eyes followed the movement with no expression. Darrell's tongue popped out on the other side of his mouth, then disappeared again. Jeremy's eyes followed the movement, then shifted to Darrell's eyes. Darrell moved his tongue again, with Jeremy watching closely. Ever so slowly, his other hand came up and he gingerly poked Darrell's lips. Darrell opened his mouth suddenly like he was going to swallow Jeremy's hand whole, eliciting a giggle from the toddler.

Darrell stood up and took Jeremy's hand. He stopped suddenly and looked down at them in astonishment. "Hey, we didn't eat supper yet! Let's go do that first before looking at the horses!"

Later, Darrell dished up ice cream while his mother and Mrs. Mac fussed over the boys, then took them in to watch television until they both fell asleep. Dorine slipped their shoes off and settled them more comfortably on the wide sofa, covering them with an afghan.

"I hope Robin will forgive me for not undressing them," she whispered as they slipped out of the room.

Marci laid her hand on Dorine's arm. "My dear, I wish I had a dollar for every time I let my boys sleep in their clothes—it's too much stress to deal with fussiness when you're just as tired as they are!"

Sitting next to the phone, Mrs. Mac joined them in alternating prayer with reading passages out of the scriptures, then, giving into weariness, the two older women retired for the night.

It was quiet when they'd left the room and Dorine glanced at

Darrell to see him regarding her speculatively. "Stop staring at me!" she muttered. His eyes brimmed with laughter but they both jumped when the phone rang. Darrell answered it. For a few seconds Dorine held her breath.

His face relaxed into a broad smile and she slumped in the chair—*it was good news!* After he hung up, he relayed that the doctor and ambulance had been waiting at the airport and they got the baby to the hospital where she was responding. Dean wanted to get a room for Melody and Robin, but they refused to leave the baby's side. Depending on how Kimberly was doing in the morning, they would fly home sometime tomorrow.

He smiled as he hung up the phone, then they gave praise and thanksgiving for doctors, hospitals, planes...and Dean.

That night in her private prayers, Dorine thanked God for providing such a strong, take-charge man to do His footwork tonight. She was overjoyed at his request for her to pray! She hugged her pillow in anticipation of seeing him again—less than two months ago, she'd been ready to spit nails about his bossiness and control. Now she could hardly wait until he returned!

Early in the morning, Dorine woke with a start—*there was no one to open the Sweet Schoppe*! She bounded out of bed and dressed quickly, hearing Darrell going downstairs. She followed him and tiptoed into the living room where the boys were sleeping soundly. Rushing into the kitchen, she said, "Darrell, I'm going in to open up for Robin. Will you keep an ear open for the boys in case they wake up before your mother gets up?"

He poured a cup of coffee and glanced at her over the rim. "Sure, no problem." He sauntered to the table and sat down.

"Are you sure you can handle this?" she asked skeptically, picking up her purse. "You're still not supposed to lift anything heavy!"

"Piece a cake," he waved. "Go on...I'll feed them so much junk food they'll bounce off the walls." He reached for the paper.

Dorine hesitated, but at his look, she shrugged and ran out to her car. Marci would take over when she got up and the little ones would be safe from Darrell's idea of a healthy diet!

Once at the café, she turned on the grill and made coffee, glad that she'd helped Robin often enough to know where everything was. Several ranchers were the first in, not totally surprised to see Dorine, but frowning in concern as she told them about the baby while taking their orders. The café was soon filled with hungry customers and Dorine rather enjoyed "slinging hash." Even when she made a few mistakes followed by good-natured laugher, she said, "So fire me!"

She was hurriedly mixing up another batch of pancake batter when Pastor Rick appeared at the kitchen door. He reached for an apron and beamed at her. "I was champion flapjack flipper in the Army!"

A flood of affection for her small town's care of its own swamped her, and she vowed fiercely once again never to leave! "I've always said we don't need a newspaper here—how did you know they're not back yet?"

He picked up the spatula and advanced on the grill. "I was over at the house yesterday and prayed with them, then called the hospital last night." Pouring the batter into smooth rounds, he added, "I should have been here sooner this morning but couldn't get out of the bed—the spirit was willing but the flesh was weak!" They laughed together and Dorine left him to the hotcakes while she put more sausages on the grill.

When she called to see how the boys were, the laughter and screaming in the background told her volumes. "What's going on?!!"

"I told you this would be a piece a cake, and that's what we're having for breakfast," Darrell quipped breathlessly.

"Darrell, don't you dare!" Knowing how he loved to get a rise out of her, she refused the bait and asked instead, "Have you heard from Dean or the hospital this morning?"

"Yea—hey! Get down off the table!" His voice faded, then came back. "Dean said the baby spent a good night and the doctor is pretty sure she could go home today."

"Praise the Lord! Did they say what it was?" At another scream from the other end of the phone, she added, "I cannot imagine what is going on there or what Mrs. Mac is going to say when she sees what's happening in her kitchen...where did you say she was?"

"I didn't say, but they're out in the garden hoeing before it gets too hot...hey, you guys! Don't throw food!—I gotta go, Dorine, the natives are restless!" He hung up and she smiled. He was in over his head, but wouldn't admit it. Passing on the good news, she returned to cooking and waiting on customers.

As word spread about the baby, more people than usual came to eat breakfast. Everyone was concerned about "their" baby. About mid-morning, a large glass jar appeared on the counter—by noon, it was half full of bills and coins.

That afternoon, a plane buzzed the town and Dorine knew it was Dean letting them know he was home. The two teens who had come to work before noon assured her that they could handle everything if she wanted to go, and she gratefully thanked them.

Driving faster than she should have, she made it back to the ranch in record time and braked in front of the house. Running up the walk, she burst into the kitchen, where the group of women sat around the table with coffee and pastries. Dean and Darrell leaned against the sink nursing mugs of coffee while they watched in amusement as Robin's boys climbed all over her. Dorine's heart gave a leap of joy when Dean glanced at her, his eyes glowing with a loving tenderness.

Melody held Kimberly over her shoulder, gently patting her back as Robin exclaimed, "It's so-o good to come home to my boys! Dorine, thanks for opening up for me this morning."

Dorine shrugged as she walked around to peer into the sleeping baby's adorable face. "It wasn't anything, that's what friends are for. We were broadcast central all morning. People came in who normally don't, wanting to hear about 'our' baby." She dropped a kiss on the slumbering child. "Did they find out what it was?"

Melody's voice wobbled a little. "They were baffled but said that small children often run high fevers for no reason at all, then it goes down and they have no idea what caused it...Thanks so much, Dorine, you'll never know how much it meant to have you helping out." She squeezed Dorine's hand.

After they'd related their experiences, the two women gathered their things and as Dorine walked to the door with them, she glanced at Dean. He tilted his head towards his den, letting her know he would be waiting for her.

She hoped her friends didn't think she was rushing them on their way, but could hardly wait for Robin to fasten the boy's seatbelts and say their farewells. Robin gave her a long, knowing look before slamming her door and starting the pickup. "You better get back in there, he was antsy all the way back…and I think I know why!" She winked broadly and drove off.

# CHAPTER FOURTEEN

Dorine hurriedly pushed open the door to the den and with no hesitation, ran into Dean's open arms. He held her tightly, resting his cheek against her temple. "I can't believe we're finally alone," he sighed softly but she could hear the weariness in his voice.

"You must be pretty tired, did you get any sleep at all?" she asked as she closed her eyes, relishing the closeness. She tightened her arms around his waist, laying her head on his chest.

"I didn't sleep much, but the thought of coming home to you kept me going." Dorine's knees went weak at the tenderness of his words, and she drew back to look up into his warm eyes. When he put his hands on either side of her face, butterflies danced in her stomach and her heart faltered, then began thudding heavily. He slowly brushed his mouth over her forehead, her nose and each cheek before whispering, "I love you—I love you—I love you." Then his lips were on hers and her eyes closed as she savored the sweet warmth. The world receded and all she knew was his touch, his familiarity, his strength. He groaned softly, moving his lips up along her cheek. "I've been wanting to do this again, ever since I kissed you the first time," he murmured softly. "That kiss the night of your party knocked my socks off!" He breathed raggedly, his heart thundering.

"Me too," she murmured, her eyes still closed. Then a frown creased her brow as her eyes opened. "But why did you act so distant afterwards? I thought I'd done something wrong." Lowering her eyes, she added hesitantly, "I know I'm not very experienced."

Pressing her close, he tucked her against his chest. "Thank heavens for that! But you didn't do anything wrong, sweetheart, it was *me*—I was afraid my desire would get out of hand. I wanted to tell you how much I love you, but it wasn't the right time... your house had just been vandalized.... and you still didn't trust me...." he drew back and looked intensely into her eyes. "I thought I was protecting you from me, and all I did was hurt you...my poor little sweetheart." He gathered her close again before continuing. "I've never felt uncertain or confused in my whole life, *but I sure am with you*! All these years of knowing you and all of a sudden, I don't know you at all. You arrived home from college, a determined *woman* with strong ideas of what you wanted to do...I felt left out, because even though you've argued about everything, you'd always told me what was going on....this time, you didn't!" He put his finger under her chin and raised her face, studying her expression. "I've loved you for so long...I can't believe you've never guessed...I thought you would, after the jackass I made of myself when you dated Steve in high school."

Dorine smiled in remembrance as she recalled the night Dean had caught her and Steve, along with two other couples, swimming in one of his cattle reservoirs. And even though they were decently clothed, he hadn't minced any words as he'd angrily listed the temptations they were courting.

"Have you been a jackass?" she daringly teased. Then her smile faded. "Dean, I've never been serious about *anyone*...until now. I've waited on the Lord about that decision, but it seems that love was right here under my nose...all the time." She touched her lips to the corner of his mouth, but he hesitated and she paused.

"Speaking of God, I've got something to tell you..." he shifted away from her slightly, taking a deep breath and squaring his shoulders.

Dorine's heart almost stopped—the one barrier that stood between them now threatened her happiness. But in the next heartbeat, she knew she could never give up her faith, never betray her love for her Lord above *any* earthly commitments. She steeled herself, waiting for the words that would destroy her dreams.

He paused, his fingers playing with the bracelet he'd given her, his eyes thoughtful. "After we left yesterday, all I could see was that last look you gave me—I wanted to *forget* everything, turn around and come back to you. But I knew Robin and Melody were depending on me. I saw the fear in Melody's eyes and when I reached over to touch the baby, I was shocked at how hot she felt. I glanced at Robin and her eyes were filled with confidence...all of a sudden, I had three people depending on me for help…and… I've never felt so *helpless* in all my life…" he moved restlessly as he admitted, "I even started to pray…" he pulled her close and rested his cheek on her hair again as he struggled with emotion.

She held her breath. *Dean had been praying?*

He continued, as though reading her thoughts. "Yeah, big ole macho cowboy," his voice was laced with derision. "I can ride a bronc into the ground, I snap my fingers and dozens of people jump…but…" his voice dropped to a whisper, "but I couldn't help that baby girl…" He began rubbing her back as his confession poured out. "I've been 'playing' at church the past few months…I did it to impress you and please Mom…but I found I was wrestling more with God than I ever did with an ornery ole steer!" He stilled and took a deep breath. "I found myself promising God all kinds of things if He'd help Kimberly… and I heard Robin praying while Melody cried real soft… I don't know if I expected a miracle right then or not, but when nothing happened that instant, the old resentment and anger toward God came flooding back. I began thinking that I was a *fool* to pray to a God that couldn't hear or didn't care." He shifted restlessly. "Then…it was so strange…I can't explain it…but…suddenly, there was a peacefulness," he shook his head in wonderment, gently rocking her from side to side. "I felt it almost tangibly, and I knew it was of God, Dorine, and I knew He'd heard Robin's prayers…maybe mine too." He lifted his hand and trailed the back of his fingers down her cheek. "I feel sort of like I did when I first accepted Christ. By the time we landed, Kimberly's fever had gone down." He cupped her cheek. "And I know Who did it."

As he laid out his feelings, Dorine's despair turned to hope, then blossomed into full joy at his confession. "I know too," she whispered softly, tears brimming her eyes. "I've been praying *so* long for you to trust God again, to come back to Him!"

"Thank you for not giving up on me, sweetheart—I've been so cold to Him for so long, I feel like the prodigal son," Dean admitted.

"Dean, God has *always* been there, waiting for you. He never moved…*you* did…He's truly the 'hound of heaven,' and He's lovingly been waiting for your return to Him." He studied her expression for a moment, then nodded slightly and lowered his head, reverently touching his lips to her closed eyelids, first one, then the other.

The phone's strident ringing caused them both to jump. He whispered, "Don't answer it."

"It might be important."

"Nothing is as important as you," he breathed as his mouth found hers again in a sweet kiss. She longed for more but knew they had to call a halt. "Dean, we have to stop!" she breathed raggedly, turning her head as the phone rang again.

Groaning in frustration, he reached over to pick up the receiver while keeping one arm around her. "Hello!" he barked. After listening a moment, he spoke forcefully. "No, I don't want to do that....because it's personal, that's why...look, I don't want to be rude, but I said no, and that's final." He hung up and tightened his hold around her waist.

She didn't resist him, but knew that they had to steer away from the direction they were heading. Even though her whole being was centered on him, her curiosity surfaced. "Who was that?"

He spoke softly into her hair. "One of the television stations in Rapid. And stop trying to change the subject—we're finally on the same wave length here!"

By a supreme effort, she forced her thoughts away from the desire that threatened to engulf her. She took a deep breath, clearing her mind. "But what does a TV station want with you?" She gently pushed away from him, putting space between them.

He sighed in resignation, even knowing she was right to call a halt. "They heard about us flying to the hospital last night and think it would make a good human interest story."

The phone rang again and he glared at it.

Dorine laughed shakily. "I'll get it this time....Hello?" Her eyes found Dean's. "Boy, they don't waste any time do they?!....Okay, I'll tell him...bye," she said fondly and put the receiver down. "That was Hazel, she says radio and television stations are running the story about the 'hero' from Silverdale who risked his life to fly a plane blindly through the night to get a sick baby to the hospital in time."

Dean groaned and ran his hands over his face, making a raspy sound against his whiskers. "Too bad it isn't winter, they would have had us braving a raging blizzard too!"

She laughed outright and leaned against his chest, watching his frustrated expression. "I love you," she said softly, kissing his chin.

He searched her eyes, drawing her close to him. "I'll never get tired of hearing that!" He paused, "And, as much as I love holding you, this is *not* a good idea!" He looked meaningfully at her and she blushed, quickly pushing out of his arms. He laughed. "Tell the rest of them that I'm going to catch a few hours sleep, and unless the house is on fire, don't wake me!"

She reached up to touch his lips lightly with hers, smiled tenderly at the warm glow in his eyes, and prudently left the room.

The phone rang constantly after that. Besides neighbors, there were several radio and television stations that wanted to interview the "hero." She gave them all a "no comment" answer, took down numbers and said Dean would call them back if he was interested.

Darrell came in from the office later, saying that Jackie, "the TV woman," had been on the phone but wouldn't take no for an answer when he said that Dean wasn't interested in an interview. Mrs. Mac clucked over inconsiderate people, but Marci proudly smiled.

Darrell grinned mischievously as he said, "Jackie's crew is on their way to set up on location in town—she wants Dean there at seven."

"I'm starved!" Dean said coming down the stairs, freshly showered and shaved, sniffing the air appreciatively as he walked across the room and wrapped his arms around Dorine. "Not just for food either!" Although she was delighted with his openness, she was embarrassed too and glanced self-consciously at Marci.

For a moment no one moved, then a beautiful smile curved Marci's lips as she came to put her arms around both of them. Mrs. Mac took a casserole out of the microwave and carried it to the table, muttering, "Just so you watch what goes on in my kitchen...but it's about time!" she gave them a watery smile before turning her back and pretended to do something at the sink.

"You guys finally figured it out!" Darrell crowed as he came to the table and stood watching them, his face reflecting his pleasure. "I've known for months!" Then he rubbed his hands together and said, "Let's eat!"

"So much for *your* romantic soul!" Dorine chided him.

"Strange," Marci said as she tipped her head back to look up at her elder son. "I always thought it would be Darrell and Dorine...."

Darrell choked, gasped theatrically and clutched his chest. "*Me*?!! Do I look like I have a death wish?!!" Dorine childishly stuck her tongue out at him while everyone laughed as they sat down for the blessing. For the first time, Dean reached for Dorine's hand in prayer before bowing his head, and her heart overflowed with happiness.

Dishing up the casserole, Darrell passed it along as he told Dean about Jackie's call and where he was expected to be that evening.

Dean stared at him for a moment, then a look of resignation came over him as he let out a long sigh. He picked up his fork and moved the food around on his plate. "All right, I guess I'll have to go—might as well get it over with; if I don't, they'll just keep after me." He slanted Dorine a glance. "You're coming with me."

"There you go again, *telling* me instead of asking me!" she said, only half-joking.

"Okay, okay, I'm sorry...force of habit...will you do the honor of accompanying me?" he replied with saccharine sweetness. She raised a skeptical eyebrow.

"Oh *brother*!" Darrell got up to take his plate to the sink. "Is there any dessert?"

Shortly before seven, Dean and Dorine arrived in Silverdale, to find a crowd of people, cars and the television van with its cameras, cables and crew. "Look at this circus!" he said under his breath, parking some distance away on the usually deserted street.

Dorine's eyes were wide with amazement. "Everyone in the

whole county must be here!" she exclaimed as she looked over the crowd. "How did they know the television crew would be here?"

"I don't know but I hate this," he muttered, sliding a finger under the bolo tie to loosen it. "Why do they have to make such a fuss?"

She patted his cheek. "Stop grumbling—you're the hero now, so act like one." He looked gorgeous to her in his western suit and white hat, tilted jauntily back so that one wayward curl escaped. She reached up to push it back and whispered, "A very sexy hero!"

He caught her hand and brought it to his mouth for a quick kiss. "I forgot my red cape." His eyes hungrily devoured her.

"Go, Sir Lancelot, your adoring public awaits you."

His eyes glittered. "You're getting your heroes mixed up—and you're enjoying this, aren't you?" She wasn't successful in hiding a giggle. "Well, if I have to do it, you're going along!" he gritted out as they got out of the car and he took her arm. He pasted on a tight smile when Jackie came to meet them.

The glamorous anchorwoman barely gave Dorine a glance, taking Dean's other arm in a calculated move. Giving direction in her well-modulated voice, she impressively moved people around and Dorine had to admire the way the other woman handled people—*everything* was orchestrated. The only time Dorine felt a twinge of jealousy was when Jackie moved close to Dean, whispering intimately. He listened courteously while she touched his shoulder and laughed merrily, gesturing towards the spotlighted area in front of the cameras. Dean turned, winking at Dorine before positioning himself next to Robin, Melody and Paul, who was lovingly cuddling Kimberly.

The gathered crowd quieted as the two women talked first, and Kimberly smiled her sweetest. Dean smoothly answered Jackie's questions in a relaxing manner that was at odds with the set of his jaw that told Dorine he would rather be anywhere than there.

Then it was over, the lights went off and the crew started rolling up their cables. As Dorine walked toward them, Jackie spotted her and deliberately slipped her hand around Dean's arm, resting it possessively there. "You all must be very proud of this big cowboy," she laughed up into his face, "he's a natural in front of the camera—are you sure you won't consider changing careers?"

Ever the gentleman, Dean didn't embarrass the woman by removing her hand, but as he gently stepped away from her, she had no course but to let her hand drop. His gaze went to Dorine, sending her a silent message of adoration. "I'd rather ride a wild bull than do that again!"

Dorine smiled confidently as he moved next to her. "Yes, we're proud of him." He put his arm around her shoulder, and after a slight hesitation, Jackie gave Dean a smile meant to exclude Dorine.

"This will be on tonight's ten o'clock news, be sure and watch!" Without another glance at Dorine, Jackie turned on her heel and strode confidently back to the television van. Robin and Melody's families were surrounded by neighbors and friends, chattering to them and each other.

"You handled that like a pro, Mr. DeFoe."

He turned to her, his eyes somber. "Dorine, she's never meant anything to me. She's made all the moves, not me."

She reached up on tiptoe to touch her lips to the corner of his mouth. "That's why I love you, you're always such a gentleman. I admire the way you handled her." They could have been the only two people in the world, unaware of others around them, cars being started, flowing into the traffic. Dean placed his hands around her waist and smiled down into her dark eyes as he looked hungrily at her lips.

"You can't kiss me here on the street," she whispered.

"There's no law against it." His eyes roved over her face.

"Everybody will see you." They leaned toward each other.

"I don't care." He closed the gap, but a blaring horn interrupted them and he turned to send a glare toward the laughing teen boy at the wheel of the car. He sighed. "I guess this *isn't* the best place."

Dorine laughed at his frustration. "Come on!" She grabbed his hand and towed him toward the knot of people in front of the Sweet Schoppe. Robin glanced up at that moment, her gaze sliding from Dorine to Dean and back again. One eyebrow rose in question. Paul drew Dean into conversation and Robin pulled Dorine to the side.

"Does this mean what I think it means?" she demanded delightedly. Her eyes twinkled as she listened to Dorine's explanation.

"Then he told me how he'd prayed for Kimberly—he actually *prayed*, Robin!" Dorine's whisper grew in excitement.

"He never said a *thing* to us!" Robin replied. "Another answer to our prayers! So." She folded her arms over her ample chest. "Does this mean wedding bells?"

"We didn't... get that far—"

"Ready to go...P.C.?" asked Dean, coming to her side. His eyes glinted with amusement as he looked down at her.

"P.C.?" Robin questioned with lifted eyebrow.

Dorine blushed. "Prairie Chick," she explained, then jabbed her elbow into Dean's side. "Let's get you out of here before you come up with any more cute names."

Over the next few days, Robin's comment about wedding bells flitted around in Dorine's head and she expectantly waited for Dean to bring up the subject of marriage. But while he stole kisses whenever he could, he never mentioned their future. Some of her excitement dimmed and she wondered if she had jumped the gun with her expectations. Doubt began to creep in, and it was confirmed a few days later.

She was sitting on the edge of his desk in the den one evening while he was on the phone—but she'd prudently left the door open.

He was confirming that the company who was going to reseal the pavement by the hanger was coming as scheduled, his fingers playing idly with hers as he talked. When he put down the phone, she slid onto his lap. Darrell chose that moment to poke his head in.

"Do you guys need a chaperone?" he teased, leaning against the doorjamb.

Dorine said, "No! Go away!" Dean sent his brother a dark look.

Darrell crossed his arms over his chest as he surveyed them with a raised eyebrow. "You better behave, or Mrs. Mac will have you at the altar with a shotgun!"

Dean stiffened and got up, letting Dorine slide off his lap. Flinging his brother an annoyed look, he growled "Buzz off!" In a matter of seconds, the atmosphere in the room had chilled. "I've got things to clear up here…I'll see you both in the morning." He dismissed them with a curtness that had Darrell grinning, but Dorine was speechless. *What in the world had come over him?!!* He stood glaring at her, no sign of the tenderness of a few moments ago.

It was clear he wanted her to leave, but her stubbornness kicked into gear before she was brought up short by what Darrell had just said. Hesitating, she tilted her chin up —why was Dean so skittish about the "marriage" word? But at the no-nonsense look in his eye, she turned on her heel and stomped out of the room. She'd always thought that he *wanted* to be married, to have children; he could hardly wait until his sister and family came so he could play with the kids. It just didn't make sense. She was reminded that her heavenly Father was waiting for her to come to Him for guidance, and she poured her heart out to Him.

# CHAPTER FIFTEEN

Dean didn't come into the office the next day, nor did she see him at meals. Her subdued demeanor had Loretta and Darlene glancing at her curiously. Hazel cast her questioning glances, exchanging looks with the other two secretaries, but no one approached her.

After supervising the job on the runway, Dean headed off to Oklahoma that same afternoon for several days of business meetings. After that, there was a snag in the arrangements for shipping stock to a rodeo in Colorado—Darrell could have gone but Dean informed Hazel he would go before returning home.

He never asked to speak with her. At the house, Marci's eyes didn't miss the symptoms of something gone amiss, but she kept her council, chatting instead about preparations for the church picnic.

Frustration began to build—Dorine really needed to talk about where this relationship was going. He could have taken her with him, especially since she had handled this particular rodeo arrangement—but he was intentionally putting distance between them. *What was wrong?*

She needed to get away to think, and as always, her mind turned towards the Badlands. For a moment, the thought of the rustlers had her hesitating but, she reasoned, they hadn't heard or seen anything for weeks, and even Bryce had dropped out of sight—she'd just keep alert and be back before anyone even knew she was gone.

Informing Hazel she was done for the day, Dorine headed for the corral after collecting her saddle pack.

Deep in thought as Blaze trotted along, she dismounted when they came to the river, and let him wade in to drink. The solitude always brought a quietness to her spirit and she felt in closer communion with God here than anywhere besides church. But today, even the droning of the insects among the reeds refused to bring that comfort. Why had Dean changed so abruptly? Blaze seemed to sense her turmoil and turned soft brown eyes on her as he put his nose against her shoulder, gently nudging her. She leaned her head against his neck, softly stroking him.

Suddenly, he jerked his head up, ears pricked forward. Water dripped off his chin as his eyes focused on hills to the north.

Dorine tensed when she saw the strange alertness of the animal. "What do you see, boy?" She turned to follow his gaze. The slanting rays of the late afternoon sun bathed the quiet countryside in soft shades of yellow and gold, but she could see nothing amiss. Whickering softly, Blaze flicked his ears back and forth. He didn't seem frightened, only curious. Using him for a barometer, Dorine decided there couldn't be trouble up the trail or he would have shown it.

Giving a tug on the reins, she urged him out of the water and mounted. He still wanted to face north, his ears twitching. She leaned forward and patted his neck. "What is it, boy?" He was motionless, and then she heard it too. A cow bawled, a distressful bawling that sounded far away. Looking at the rim of the sky, she knew it wouldn't be long till the sun slid down below the hills... she should be starting back. The cow bawled again. She couldn't leave without finding out what was wrong. If an animal *was* in trouble, she'd never forgive herself for leaving without checking.

A slight pressure of her legs had Blaze moving forward, eager to run. "Easy, boy, easy," Dorine spoke softly. She reined him in, deciding to climb the nearest incline to get a better view of what lay ahead. The thought of having to tend a sick or hurt animal in the dark had her patting the saddle pack to make sure the flashlight was there—yes, along with the phone and her gun.

She stopped near an outcropping of rocks at the top of an incline and listened. Blaze snorted and pricked his ears forward again, this time searching the horizon the same as she. There didn't appear to be anything unusual, then Dorine heard the bawling again. This time it sounded closer—and like more than one animal. She urged the horse forward, trotting down a sloping incline and galloping across a grassy meadow. Blaze climbed the next incline, coming to a stop when Dorine tightened the reins.

Just ahead, beyond the next outcropping, she spotted the red hides of the Herefords. She couldn't tell how many because they moved around in the scrub trees and were partially hidden by the outcropping. *What were they doing so far out here?*

However, since she'd promised herself she wouldn't act foolishly, she reached around into the backpack and fumbled for the cell phone, dialing the house number. To her surprise, Dean answered. She hadn't heard any planes since she'd left the ranch.

"Where are you?" he demanded brusquely. "Hazel said you left early and didn't say where you were going—didn't you check in with anyone?" She blinked—*where had the tender lover gone?*

"You're back," she stated unnecessarily, not liking his tone.

"Only to find you gone and your horse too—where are you?!!" he demanded again.

After the frustration of not being able to talk to him, his curt tones sent her irritation soaring and her chin lifted. "I'm checking a bunch of cattle north of the riv—"

"You get back here, *right now*!"

She hesitated a moment—but only a moment. *How dare he give her orders?!!* She very deliberately pressed the 'off' button. *You'd think he'd realize by now that she was her own woman!* The phone began to vibrate. He was trying to get her attention, but she smugly dropped the phone into her saddlebag and continued on her way.

Dean frantically punched redial again and again, and felt like throwing the phone across the room when she didn't answer. Fear stabbed his gut as he remembered Bryce's warnings about that almost inaccessible area north of the river...and she was headed right into it.

He jabbed in the number for his foreman, barking out orders before hurrying to the barn to saddle his horse. Good thing it was still light enough for the horses to see the trail. Throwing on the blanket and saddle, then tightening the cinch, he silently prayed for Dorine's safety—then his hands stilled. *He was praying!* And it felt *wonderful* to commune with the Father again! Resting his forehead on the saddle, clutching the edges of the leather in both hands, he closed his eyes. *Father God, I've been away from You for so long. But now I'm bowing at Your Throne of Mercy not for me, but for Dorine. Put a hedge of protection around her, Father.* As a tear squeezed out from under his eyelid, his shoulders heaved. *I've loved her for so long, I can't lose her now. Give her safety, I pray it in the Name of Your Son. Amen.*

Dorine urged Blaze forward. "Okay, old boy, let's go see what we can see, before that Dean has a cow…get it, Blaze?" she joked. The horse picked his way through the small rocks scattered about the ledge, coming around a large rock.

He stopped and snorted. She saw the mounted riders at the same time and fear clutched her heart. Cattle were milling around in a small hidden valley below, and she knew in one sweeping glance, that she'd stumbled onto the rustlers.

"Oh, *man*! Let's get out of here!" She urged the horse back, hoping to duck out of sight before the riders spotted her. Every nerve was geared for flight, but she stopped short when she saw a lone rider coming up the trail behind her—with a rifle pointed right at her.

Blaze threw his head up, snorted and began dancing sideways, almost unseating Dorine. "Whoa, boy, whoa!" she called out. His eyes were filled with fear and he moved dangerously close to the steep incline while she fought to control him, his hooves churning up dirt and dust.

It seemed only seconds before the men reached them, dismounting in a swirl of dry, powdery dust. She tried to urge Blaze forward, hoping to catch the men off-guard and bluff her way through them, but Blaze was uncontrollable with fright. Two of the men dismounted and one, a big burly man, ran to her side, grabbed her and pulled her off the horse.

"Let me go!" she yelled, kicking and hitting at him. Blaze reared and yanked the reins out of her hand, putting her off balance. She fell on the rocky ground, pain snaking up her leg. But she was up immediately, ready to defend herself. Her heart was pounding and she tasted fear through the dryness in her throat. The man put his sinewy arms around her from behind while she used her feet to kick at his legs. "Let…me….go!" she yelled.

He laughed. "Boy, what a wildcat!" Easily holding her prisoner, the big man watched his companions trying to get her horse under control. Blaze was still rearing and tossing his head, so terrified that his eyes rolled back to show the whites. He snorted and whistled, trying to get away as two of the mounted riders twirled their ropes. "Stop! Don't hurt him!" Dorine cried out, still struggling.

The first man that had dismounted seemed to be the leader. "Quit fighting, and we won't hurt the horse!" he snapped at her. She gradually stilled, watching as the ropes settled on her horse's neck and the men rode off a ways, dragging Blaze behind, still snorting and trying to rear.

She turned pleading eyes to the leader. "Don't hurt him!" She was struck by his fancy "dude" clothes—expensive Stetson hat, bolo tie with a western shirt and dress pants. She took grim satisfaction that his once shiny boots were now covered with the fine powdery dust.

He was returning her assessment with a cool, pale blue gaze. "There, now that's better. You must be Ms. Andrews," he sneered. "You should have listened to Alfred when he told you not to come out here."

*Alfred! What did he—?* With sinking heart, it all fell into place, why her cousin was so adamant about her not coming to the ranch—he was mixed up with these men!

"Tie her hands!" The leader barked at the man holding her. When he let go of her to reach for a rope, Dorine tried to run, but slipped and fell. "I wouldn't try that again," smirked the leader, nodding at the man with the rifle. "He can pick you off before you'd get ten feet!"

She stood up slowly, turning to look at the rider who appeared to be about her age, but she'd never seen him before. He tipped his black hat back and gave her a cocky grin when she glared angrily. He laughed and dismounted. "Whatcha gonna do with her?" he asked in a suggestive voice. "She looks like she could be fun—"

"Don't even think it!" snapped the leader, turning away from Dorine. "Get back up on that horse and go keep watch. As soon as they know she's missing, they'll be out here!" He swore roundly, kicking at a sagebrush as he went back to his horse. Rough rope was tied tightly around Dorine's wrists, with her hands in front of her.

"Not so tight!" she cried out. The burly man laughed and imitated her. "Not so tight!" He jerked on the rope to make sure it was tight, noticing her bracelet. His eyes widened as he touched it. "Ni-c-e," he drawled. She jerked away and he laughed nastily.

The other men had succeeded in bringing Blaze under control, but the leader ordered the burly man to put Dorine on a different horse and blindfold her. "No!" she tried to reach up to scratch her abductor. His smile faded when he realized her intentions. He caught her arms, swearing, then raised a beefy hand and backhanded her across the face.

Her head exploded with pain and a misty darkness lurked behind her eyes. Her knees buckled and she thought she'd fall, but her captor's beefy arm kept her from falling.

"Cut that out!' yelled the leader. "We don't have time for that!" She could taste blood and licked her lips, trying to focus her eyes. Her abductor whipped out a black kerchief and tied it over her face, then she was lifted into the saddle. Unable to see, she gripped the saddle horn with her bound hands, willing herself not to topple over. Her jaw stung from the slap and she ran her tongue around the inside of her mouth. *Dear Lord, what had she gotten herself into?!! Heavenly Father, protect me!*

"Let's git outta here!" The horse moved forward, and she heard whistles and shouts, as the men apparently began moving the cattle. *Lord Jesus, help me in my time of trouble. I know I've been stubborn and willful, forgive me for being wayward. Perhaps you've put Dean into my life as a guide and I failed to see it through my stubbornness...guide him to me...I'm helpless without your protection. Keep me safe through this!* Alternating between silent prayer and berating herself, she felt the air grow cooler, indicating the sun had gone down. Her jaw ached and she could still taste blood.

It was a long time before they stopped and she was dragged roughly out of the saddle. Feeling groggy and disoriented as she was shoved forward, she almost fell. "Put her in there!" ordered the leader's voice.

She was lifted in sweaty arms, could hear the sound of the man's boots swishing through the grass, then step up, thumping on a wood floor. She was dropped none too gently to the floor and the bandanna was removed. Twilight shadows made it hard to focus but she could see they were inside an old line shack. The burly man leaned over with another rope, which he tied around her legs. Flashlights bobbed around outside, and she could hear the men talking.

"What are you going to do with me?" she looked up into the man's face, obscured in the darkness. He laughed and turned away, going out the door. She moved her wrists, and the rope cut deeper into them. She wondered if she could bite through them and had to stifle hysterical laughter at the thought of gnawing the rope like a dog.

Thirst was drying her throat and her jaw was turning sore. She peered into the corners of the dark shack, wondering if there was anything she could use to get loose. Then she heard a familiar voice that chilled her blood.

"What're you guys doin'? How come you're way over here?"

*Alfred!*

"We got your cousin, she was snooping around again."

"You've got *Dorine*?" Alfred's incredulous voice carried to her. "Why? Looky here, kidnappin' wasn't in the deal!"

"She *saw* us, Dalton, she can identify us!"

"It was bad 'nough that ya trashed our house—"

"Shut up! We had to do something to get 'em off our trail!"

So Alfred *did* know who had vandalized the house!

After a brief silence, he hesitantly asked, "What are ya gonna do with her?"

"Haven't decided yet." Their voices sounded closer. "But we've got to get rid of her."

"Ya promised me nobody would git hurt—"

"And you promised you'd keep her out of the way!" snapped the leader. "B-u-u-t-t," he drawled, "we could let nature take its course…"

"You're not gonna just *leave* her here, are ya? It could be *days* before somebody finds her!"

"By then it could be too late...she could have died from snakebite..."

"That's murder!"

The leader's voice was cold. "Nobody could ever prove we had a *thing* to do with it." Dorine sobbed silently as she thought of a slithery, beady-eyed snake crawling over her....*oh, Dean, why didn't I listen to you? Why do I always have to be so headstrong?!! My darling, am I ever going to see you again?!!*

"Lookit here," Alfred's voice was sounding desperate, "this whole thin's gettin' outta hand—I shoulda called the deal off after ya trashed the house—now ya want to add kidnappin' and... and murder—well, I don't want no part of it!"

"Tough!" came the snarling voice of the leader. "You're up to your ears in this, Dalton!" In a silky voice, he added, "Are you telling me you want to back out of our deal? No way—all I have to do is testify that stealing cattle was *your* idea, and the boys will back me up! You'll take the rap for all of this, and the rest of us will get off easy!"

Alfred was silent, then in a weaker voice he asked, "So now what?" Their voices grew fainter as they moved away and she strained to hear them. Someone shouted, "Turn off those flashlights—from here on, we have to do this in the dark!" She heard the faint sound of vehicles in low gear, and realized they were bringing in cattle trucks.

She leaned back. *Oh, Lord, my sin of willfulness has brought me here to this place. Forgive me, Father and put your protection around me, I ask in Jesus name*— a rustling nearby halted the prayer. A snake? She gasped—*no, Lord, please not that!*

"Dorine? Ps-s-t! Don't make a sound if you can hear me." *It was Alfred!* She could barely make out his faint shadow in the doorway.

"Alfred? What are you going to do? *Why* have you done this? Why? *Why?*" Her voice was choked with tears.

"Shut up! I di'nt bargain for *this*." He reached out to touch her on the shoulder. She flinched and jerked back from his hand.

"Bargained for what? What are you doing?" she whispered louder.

"Sh-h! Keep your voice down," he warned.

"Can't you even untie me?"

"No...I gotta think of a way to git ya outta this without them suspectin' me. Otherwise, I'll be no help to ya."

"Alfred, I can't believe that you're doing this—does Vicki know?"

He stifled a short, mirthless laugh. "No, as long as I keep her in clothes and hair dye, she's happy."

"Alfred, to steal cattle like this—" she choked back a sob and looked up at him. "Why? I know things aren't so good, but—"

"It's a long story, and I can't go inta it now. We gotta git ya out of here—do ya still carry that cell phone?"

"Yes, it's in my pack, but how are you going to get it? They've probably gone through the backpack—and my gun! Alfred, my *gun* is in that pack!"

"Sh-h, I'll try to git to that phone. Ya jest sit tight."

"Don't leave me here like this!"

There was a rustling sound as he stood up. "And don't *you* do anythin' foolish—I got us inta this mess and I'll git us out." He moved away, his shadow disappearing out the door.

"Dear Jesus, be with Alfred," she prayed in a whisper. "We're both in a big mess and need Your protection. Please watch over us and turn the hearts of those men out there, I ask it in Your precious name." A tear trickled down her cheek as she lifted her face heavenward, waiting....waiting... then, a familiar, quiet peace settled over her and she felt surrounded by a Heavenly Presence as the fear subsided.

She was in *His* care now, and whatever happened to her would be in *His* plans.

She was just whispering a quiet "Amen," when her ears picked up a distant sound. It was faint, but a distinct "whop-whop" sent shivers down her spine. A helicopter! Was God sending help already? "Even before ye ask, He is answering," came the scripture. Encouraged, she thrashed her legs, trying to loosen the ropes.

Determined to stand, she pushed herself backwards across the dirty floor until her back came up against rough boards. Bracing her feet, she pushed hard, sliding up the wall, feeling slivers embedding themselves in her shirt. She fell twice before gaining her feet, then hopped to the door.

Outside, pandemonium had broken out—men were cursing, then shots rang out and the helicopter sounded closer. A bright spotlight beamed down from above, and an authoritative voice over a loudspeaker directed the milling men to throw down their guns. Dorine blinked at the bright light, trying to adjust her eyes as she leaned against the doorway.

Those men…she blinked again, and saw shadowy forms moving into the light, holding rifles on her abductors. Recognizing Dean's ranch hands, a sob escaped as relief flooded through her.

One of the shadowy figures detached itself from the others— *Dean!* She sagged against the door, watching as he ran to a smaller figure and grabbed him by the shirtfront. Dorine squinted— Alfred! And he was gesturing wildly towards the shack. Dean shoved him backwards so hard he fell, but Dean never looked back.

"Dean! Dean! I'm here!" she cried out hoarsely, tears running down her cheeks as she sank onto the floor, her legs suddenly giving out.

In seconds, she was scooped up in his strong arms, while he breathed raggedly, "Dorine! Oh, sweetheart!" He said her name over and over, clutching her to his chest. "I was so afraid!!" He loosened his hold only long enough to untie her wrists and deftly whipped the ropes from her ankles. He lifted his gaze and searched her face in the flickering shadows. "Did they hurt you?"

"No, I'm alri—"

"Look at your face! What did they *do* to you? Who did it?" his voice turned murderous as his hand tenderly cupped her chin.

"I'm all right," she whispered weakly, leaning into him.

Clasping her again, he buried his face in her hair. "I'm *never* letting go of you again!" he murmured shakily.

"You found her!" Bryce appeared out of the confusion, a rifle in one hand. "Is she okay?" He peered at Dorine with an anxious expression.

Dean nodded without looking at him, then raised his head. "As soon as I get my hands around Alfred's neck, I'm going to—"

"No!" Dorine cried out. "He was the one who called you, he tried to make them let me go!"

Dean gazed down at her. "Nobody called us, Dorine, except you—and if you hadn't told me where you were, we would never have found you—why did you turn your phone off?" he asked incredulously. "We left as soon as we could get saddled—it's a good thing the horses knew the way in the dark. After we met Bryce, he said he'd seen the rustlers take you prisoner..." he stopped and choked, unable to go on at the horrible images he had conjured up during the long hours of the night. He trembled so violently Dorine thought he might drop her.

"How *did* you get out here so fast, with all these men...and the helicopter?" She turned to Bryce.

"I'd had the rustlers under observance for quite awhile, then when they grabbed you, I had no choice but to move my units in. What were you *doing* so far out there?"

Dean held up his hand. "There's time enough for questions later—let's get her out of here, she's going to need a doctor."

Dorine made a faint sound, and with a quick glance at her white face, Dean scooped her up again. "I'm okay," she tried to reassure him but she was suddenly very cold and her teeth began to chatter.

Bryce nodded. "She's probably going into shock, we need to keep her warm. Get a blanket over here!" he shouted. Bringing a small radio to his mouth, he spoke into it, and the helicopter began descending. Some distance away, it hovered before settling, sending dust churning upwards in big clouds. Shadowy figures hunched their shoulders against the dust as Dean carried Dorine under the moving blades and climbed into the helicopter.

"What's going to happen to them?" Dorine asked, her mouth

feeling like it was full of cotton.

Dean rapped out, "Hang 'em all, I hope!" He lowered her into a seat. The copter immediately lifted up and Dorine sank into the seat, relief finally flooding through her. She felt Dean fasten the seatbelt around her, his warm arms holding her as she sank into oblivion.

# CHAPTER SIXTEEN

She stirred when the helicopter landed in Rapid City, becoming increasingly aware of discomforting pain—her face, her wrists, her legs. She whimpered and moved her head.

"Sh-h-h," Dean murmured, gently stroking her hair. He'd faced a thousand demons tonight and knew without a doubt that his precious Dorine was here alive only because of God's loving care.

"I hurt," she whispered.

"I know, honey, I know," came his deep comforting voice.

Dean had cradled her the whole trip, his eyes seldom leaving her face. *That poor swollen face.* His jaw clenched in anger. He'd *kill* whoever did this to her!

The waiting hospital staff whisked her away, allowing him to follow her gurney into the emergency room. When they were alone, she looked up at him. "Dean, I'm so sorry—"

"Sh-h-h," he leaned over her. "It's okay—"

"No, it's not!" Tears trickled from the corners of her eyes. "Please let me say this, Dean. I've been so stubborn and wrong. I had a lot of time to think when I was in that shack, and I realized that you and Bryce, and even Alfred, were only trying to protect me. I've been so unfair to you. Please forgive me."

He slid his arms behind her shoulders and lifted her against him, burying his face in her hair. "Yes," he murmured, his own eyes smarting, "you're forgiven, sweetheart, a thousand times. But I was at fault too, for coming on so strong all the time…I need to ask your forgiveness for that." He drew back and looked at her. She nodded her head and was about to speak when the curtains around them parted and a doctor came in to examine her.

After having x-rays, which thankfully showed no broken bones, the doctor assured them that the swelling on her face would go down in a few days. "She'll have one doozer of a shiner, though!" The doctor's eyes left the chart in his hand and drifted over the tall cowboy whose face was lined with worry. He turned back to Dorine.

"Someone will be in to bandage those wrists, then you can go. You should see your own doctor in about a week, unless you notice redness, then go right away."

"Thanks, Doc," Dean shook the doctor's hand, who turned and disappeared between the green curtains billowing around the bed.

Dean chose to leave while the nurses bandaged Dorine's wrists, going to the vending machine for coffee. Ambling over to look out the window toward the brightening eastern sky, he saw the still-slumbering city below, peacefully unaware of the drama that had played out that night.

Peace. He'd struggled with anger all night, knowing it was unproductive, but it was difficult—especially every time he looked at Dorine's face. The unseen sun heralded its soon-arrival beyond the horizon with brighter and bolder light, promising a new day, a new start. "God, help me work through this anger and give *me* peace, a new start." As the bright rim of the sun peeked above the horizon, soft gold and pink washed over the sky and with it came a slow release of his anger as he handed it up to God. He became aware of wakening birds' chirruping and wondered again why the stupid little creatures would choose to nest in the city instead of a quiet countryside. Gazing towards the Badlands, he wondered how Bryce and the police were doing with the rustlers. Darrell had wanted to stick with Bryce, but realized Dean and Dorine had no way home so he was now on the way to Rapid to pick them up in the car.

Hearing soft voices, Dean turned to see Dorine walking beside the nurse towards him.

"Here she is, as good as new!" chirruped the nurse. She smiled at Dorine and handed her a slip of paper. "This is a prescription doctor left for you in case you have pain."

"Thanks," Dorine smiled gratefully.

"Take care now!" The nurse glided swiftly away and disappeared into the next cubicle.

"You're sure you feel well enough to go home?" Dean asked anxiously, hovering over her. He put the cup down, reaching for her.

"Yes. I'm okay except for feeling a little shaky."

"Let's go sit in the waiting area until Darrell gets here." He took her arm and gently led her to an overstuffed chair. "Want some coffee?" At her nod, he went to the vending machine and returned with coffee.

She took a sip and closed her eyes in bliss. "You know me so well," she murmured. The coffee, sweetened just the way she liked it, slid down her throat to sooth it. Dean's thoughtfulness again caused guilt to overwhelm her.

"What?" he asked, watching her closely.

She reached over and put one hand on his. "I don't think I can ever forgive myself for how foolish I acted today."

"It was yesterday, and stop beating yourself up about it. You're safe and that's all that matters now. I really want to kiss you but your face must be as sore as the dickens."

Suddenly she tensed. "What about Blaze! Where is he?"

"Everything's taken care of, sweetheart," he soothed her. "Bryce and Darrell are on top of things."

She relaxed, laying her head back. She should know by now that Dean would have thought of everything that mattered to her. "Dean, how could Alfred get mixed up in something like this?"

"I don't know, but I've suspected something for a long time." He idly lifted her hand and played with her fingers.

She gazed at his dear face. He'd always been looking out for her and she'd done nothing but thrown his love back at him. How could he be so forgiving? Then she remembered...he was finally trusting God again. A slow smile spread over her face but she winced when a pain shot up her cheek. She raised a hand to gingerly touch her cheek. "I'll bet I look awful, like I've been in a fight."

"Yeah, but you oughta see the other guy!" Dean kidded gently. Her eyes wouldn't meet his. "You're still gorgeous, my little prairie chick," he assured her.

"Yeah, and pigs fly."

His chuckle had her glancing at him. "It's good to hear some spunk from those sweet lips." His mouth gently grazed her other cheek.

After they were back at the ranch, Dean was like a hawk, watching her every move, with Marci and Mrs. Mac hovering tenderly around her. She never felt so pampered and special in all her life.

But something continued to bother her—Dean never said anything about their future. He was always so loving and attentive, but it seemed he was living just for the day. Didn't thoughts of marriage usually follow a declaration of love? She was completely bewildered.

Jackie had done an in-depth story about the rustlers and Dorine's kidnapping, but this time she honored Dean's request not to put them before the cameras because of Dorine's traumatic experience. Dorine would have to testify at the trial, but because Alfred had told the police everything, there was a chance the judge would go lightly on him. He would still have to serve some prison time, and Dorine was sorry for that—he'd been caught up in the greedy scheme because he had weakly given into pressure. Fortunately, none of the hands were involved, even though several of them had suspicions that something wasn't right. Alfred had written a simple, short note asking her forgiveness and she'd written back that she did forgive him, and would be praying for both him and Vicki. From Vicki, they heard nothing.

Bryce told her she could move back to her house and when Dean suggested hiring a cleaning service to go in first, she agreed and lined up a company from Rapid City.

Now that she was feeling better, she grew restless and knew the best remedy was work—to which Dean reluctantly agreed. The day he found her with an oil can heading for his squeaky office chair, he smiled indulgently, but there was a troubled look about him. "When you get through there, come over to the barn."

She'd expected him to enjoy her joke at greater length, but at his somber command, her smile faded and she took little joy in oiling the chair that had driven her nuts for the past several months.

When she rounded the corner of the barn, he had Blaze and Black saddled. Wordlessly, he handed her the reins and mounted his horse. They rode towards the Badlands, but Dorine didn't venture any questions after noting Dean's troubled expression. She never seen a less-loverlike expression—*What was wrong?*

After some time, they came to a high outcropping overlooking the trail. "Leave the horses here," he commanded, dismounting. She slid from the saddle, dropping the reins, and the horses began grazing.

Dean held out his hand and she silently took it. His strong grip sent a thrill through her, but apprehension tempered the feeling.

They climbed slowly to the top, where he gestured for her to sit down. While she caught her breath, he began pacing back and forth, took his hat off, ran his fingers through his hair and rammed the hat back on. Stopping a little ways from her, he gave a heavy sigh and tucked his fingers in his front pockets, gazing out over the Badland's grandeur.

Then he raised one hand and rubbed the back of his neck. His expression was now one of indecision and she could only wait patiently for him to speak. *Oh, how she loved this man!* And whatever was bothering him, she wanted to make it go away.

"Dorine..." he began hesitantly. He stopped, took a deep breath and flexed his shoulders, gazing into the distance. "I've got a confession to make, and I want your promise to stay sitting there."

She decided to try a light note. "Well, it's not like I'm going to run away from you!"

"You'll probably *want* to, after you hear what I have to say." He looked at the ground and spoke so quietly, she could barely hear him. "Your dad never gave you that trust fund to go to college." Trying to ignore her sharply indrawn breath, he grimly went on. "He had it all set up, but never got around to signing it." Pausing, he nudged a small rock with his boot tip, still not knowing quite how to confess the secret he'd kept for so long.

She searched his face, her heart pounding. "*You*...did it, didn't you?" Her first shock was dismay, followed by guilt at the way she'd treated him. That was followed by the knowledge that he'd done this out of love for her, just as he'd done everything in the past years.

He slowly nodded, avoiding her eyes. "I saw how desperate you were to go to college, but I also knew you would never accept help from anyone, least of all me." He nudged the rock again. "You'll never know how many nights I laid awake, trying to think of how to get that money to you without your knowledge…I finally went to my lawyer and asked if we could set up some kind of fund, something legal, without you knowing where it came from."

"So…so I actually owe you—"

"No!" He was beside her in three strides, whipping off his hat and dropping it before kneeling in front of her. "No! You don't owe me anything. It was meant as a gift of love!" He took her cold hands in his and held them tight, his eyes earnestly searching hers. "But I didn't wait on the Lord to work out His will, I ran ahead of Him, thinking *I* was the one to solve all your problems. I was wrong…so wrong." The bracelet softly tinkled when he touched her. He looked down at it, and gently rubbed his thumb over it. "When I gave you this bracelet, my heart was dangling at the end of it…did you know the 'D' was for 'Dean' and he was giving you his heart?"

"Who…who else knows?" she whispered. "I mean, about the trust fund?" Her eyes mirrored bewilderment.

"No one, not even Mother." He waited for her response and held his breath. *Please Lord, don't let her turn away.*

"If no one else knows, why *did* you tell me?" she said slowly. "I would never have found out, and you could have kept your secret."

He put his head down in her lap, over their hands. "Because I want a future with you, and that means being honest and open with each other. I could never face you day after day, knowing that I was living a lie. You would probably never have known, but *I* know—and I want to be as honest with you as you've always been with me." He raised his head, kneeling in the dirt at her feet—and waited.

She was still for a moment, studying his earnest expression, then pulled her hands from under his and placed them on either side of his face, her eyes softening. "I love you," she whispered. "Nothing will ever change that." He dropped his head into her lap again with a muffled groan of relief. Leaning forward, he slid his arms around her, bringing her close to him. She stroked his hair, then rested her cheek on his head, marveling at the love they had, as the fading rays of the sun blessed them in tints of peach and pink.

He drew back, reaching into his pocket. "I've been planning for the day I'd propose to you and I can't think of a better place than here at the Badlands!" He withdrew a small velvet box and opened it. Inside was a sparkling diamond that caught the light in a prism of colors. "Will you be my wife, prairie chick, will you stand together with me for the rest of our lives?" Her eyes widened at the beauty of the engagement ring and her eyes filled with tears. He quickly added, "I *couldn't* ask you before, not until I confessed…and it took me awhile to build up my courage."

"Because I always jumped all over you," Dorine added. "I'm *so* sorry, Dean!" She swallowed a sob.

"Your dad knew how I felt about you and he gave me his blessing a couple of years before he died…he knew that if anything happened to him, I would be there for you, protect you, watch over you…along with the Lord." He hesitated, then took the ring out of the box, turning questioning eyes to her. "Will you marry me, Dorine?"

She looked into the depths of the clear blue of his eyes. "Yes," she replied softly. "I'll be proud to be your wife." Very carefully, he slid the exquisite stone onto her ring finger—it fit perfectly. He kissed it tenderly. "I've wanted to ask you ever since you turned sixteen, but you had to grow up, had to experience life first. I nearly drove myself crazy wondering if you'd want to stay on the ranch…and to be a rancher's wife for the next eighty years."

When she looked up, mischief twinkled in her eyes. "Only eighty?" He swallowed and she realized her big macho man had been afraid to ask her the most important question of his life. "You must have been awfully sure of yourself to bring that ring along with you, considering you didn't know how I'd react to your confession."

He rose to his feet, bringing her up with him. "I'm *never* sure, not where you're concerned." Then he bent his head and she met him halfway. Reverently kissing her, he gathered her close, sending shivers skittering along her arms. Then a thought occurred to her, one that might give him pause before making a commitment.

She drew back and looked up into his eyes, a frown marring her forehead. "Dean?" His heart thumped. *Had she changed her mind?* "I'm learning to put *my* will aside, to let *God's* will be my guide from now on…but…I can't change my personality. I can't promise that my stubbornness won't be a problem."

He let his breath out as relief coursed through him and he attempted to draw her close again. "I don't *want* you to be any different—you're just right, stubbornness and all!"

She held him away by placing her hands on his chest. "I just want you to know that God must have given me this personality for a reason—I'll still speak my mind if I don't agree with something that you do—and I *won't* back down if I think you're wrong!"

He studied her serious face, then somberly replied, "Thank God for that—Dorine, I *need* your strength and determination to help me run this," he tilted his head toward the ranchland around them, "and this marriage will be a partnership."

Then a lazy smile spread over his face as he shook his head. "I don't know what I'm letting myself in for, do I?" Holding her close, he buried his nose in her hair. "But it sure isn't going to be dull!"

She smiled and planted a string of small kisses along his jaw. "Our partnership is a *three-way* deal…don't forget…a triangle is awfully hard to break."

He raised his head, his gaze wrapping warmly around her heart. "You, me and the Lord," he agreed, with praises singing in his heart.

# CHAPTER SEVENTEEN

At the engagement party, ranchers and neighbors from miles around came to the festive event. When everyone had eaten and gathered on the patio, Dean quieted them with his upraised hand and said, "I have a gift for my bride-to be. Some of you probably don't know this, but I actually asked Dorine to marry me when she was sixteen, and do you remember what you said?" He looked down at her, snuggled against his side with his arm around her waist. She blushed and ducked her head into his shirtfront. He chuckled. "She said that when pigs fly, she would marry me!" A burst of laughter was followed by loud applause.

Dean turned and took a flat rectangular package from Darrell, presenting it to Dorine, who eyed the package uncertainly.

It was obviously a painting, but she couldn't imagine what it could be. Carefully unwrapping it, she caught a glimpse of the subject matter and began to laugh. Turning the painting so all could see, she shared her laughter with everyone she held dear.

The painting was of the DeFoe Ranch, and flying above the house in the blue sky, were dozens of pink pigs with white wings.

**THE END**

Printed in the United States
1119800002B/40-69